NASHVILLE | PART SEVEN |COMMIT

NASHVILLE | PART SEVEN |COMMIT

INGLATH COOPER

Contents

Books by Inglath Cooper

My Italian Lover – What If – Book One
Fences
Dragonfly Summer – Book Two – Smith Mountain Lake Series
Blue Wide Sky – Book One – Smith Mountain Lake Series
That Month in Tuscany
Crossing Tinker's Knob
Jane Austen Girl
Good Guys Love Dogs
Truths and Roses
Nashville – Book Ten – Not Without You
Nashville – Book Nine – You, Me and a Palm Tree
Nashville – Book Eight – R U Serious
Nashville – Book Seven – Commit
Nashville – Book Six – Sweet Tea and Me
Nashville – Book Five – Amazed
Nashville – Book Four – Pleasure in the Rain
Nashville – Book Three – What We Feel
Nashville – Book Two – Hammer and a Song
Nashville – Book One – Ready to Reach
On Angel's Wings
A Gift of Grace
RITA® Award Winner John Riley's Girl
A Woman With Secrets
Unfinished Business
A Woman Like Annie
The Lost Daughter of Pigeon Hollow
A Year and a Day

Copyright

Commit

com·mit·ted; com·mit·ting – to carry into action deliberately. To pledge oneself to another through the good and the bad, through sickness and health. A committed love is a forever love.

Reviews

Readers who have enjoyed the emotional stories of authors like Colleen Hoover may enjoy this live-your-dream story where "Inglath Cooper draws you in with her words and her amazing characters. It is a joy to pick up these books. There is just the right amount of love and romance with the perfect dose of reality. The dialogue is relatable and you just fall in love with the story."

♪

"Truths and Roses . . . so sweet and adorable, I didn't want to stop reading it. I could have put it down and picked it up again in the morning, but I didn't want to." – **Kirkusreviews.com**

On Truths and Roses: "I adored this book…what romance should be, entwined with real feelings, real life and roses blooming. Hats off to the author, best book I have read in a while." – **Rachel Dove, FrustratedYukkyMommyBlog**

"I am a sucker for sweet love stories! This is definitely one of those! It was a very easy, well written, book. It was easy to follow, detailed, and didn't leave me hanging without answers." – **www.layfieldbaby.blogspot.com**

"I don't give it often, but I am giving it here – the sacred 10. Why? Inglath Cooper's A GIFT OF GRACE mesmerized me; I consumed it in one sitting. When I turned the last page, it was three in the morning." – **MaryGrace Meloche, Contemporary Romance Writers**

5 Blue Ribbon Rating! ". . .More a work of art than a story. . .Tragedies affect entire families as well as close loved ones, and this story portrays that beautifully as well as giving the reader hope that somewhere out there is A GIFT OF GRACE for all of us." — **Chrissy Dionne, Romance Junkies 5 Stars**

"A warm contemporary family drama, starring likable people coping with tragedy and triumph." 4 1/2 Stars. — **Harriet Klausner**

"A GIFT OF GRACE is a beautiful, intense, and superbly written novel about grief and letting go, second chances and coming alive again after devastating adversity. Warning!! A GIFT OF GRACE is a three-hanky read…better make that a BIG box of tissues read! Wowsers, I haven't cried so much while reading a book in a long long time…Ms. Cooper's skill makes A GIFT OF GRACE totally believable, totally absorbing…and makes Laney Tucker vibrantly alive. This book will get into your heart and it will NOT let go. A GIFT OF GRACE is simply stunning in every way—brava, Ms. Cooper! Highly, highly recommended!" – **4 1/2 Hearts — Romance Readers Connection**

"…A WOMAN WITH SECRETS…a powerful love story laced with treachery, deceit and old wounds that will not heal…enchanting tale…weaved with passion, humor, broken hearts and a commanding love that will have your heart soaring and cheering for a happily-ever-after love. Kate is strong-willed, passionate and suffers a bruised heart. Cole is sexy, stubborn and also suffers a bruised heart…gripping plot. I look forward to reading more of Ms. Cooper's work!" – **www.freshfiction.com**

Thomas

Chemical Romance

I'VE NEVER BEEN a morning person.

Not until Lila, that is.

In my past life — pre-Lila — I could sleep until noon if no one woke me. Now, I'm awake before she is, five-thirty, six o'clock, trying not to wake her up. But as soon as I open my eyes, it's as if she senses it, and within moments, she's awake too.

In all honesty, I think our bodies wake each other up. It's like a chemical thing. When too many hours have passed, and we haven't had each other again, alarm systems start going off inside us, demanding attention. Sounds crazy, I know, but that's what it feels like.

This morning is no exception.

I've been staring at the ceiling for sixty seconds or less when Lila starts to stretch beside me, arms raised above her head, her left leg sliding along mine, her skin like silk against me.

"Umm," she says.

My body responds instantly, and I hook an arm around her waist, pulling her over and across me. "Come here, naked woman," I say.

Her long hair drops across her shoulder like a curtain, the ends brushing my face. "You rang, naked man?"

We both laugh, and I lift my head off the pillow, kissing the side of her neck.

"You've ruined me," I say.

"How so?" she asks, her voice husky at the edges, as she studies my face.

"You're all I think about."

"And the problem is?" she teases.

"Well, it's not really a problem as long as you're handy."

"Is this handy?" she asks, moving against me.

A knife of desire hits me so hard that I can't breathe for a second. "Very," I say, flipping her over and under me.

It's a good while before either of us says anything else. Words aren't remotely necessary for us to express what we feel.

A little later, I brush her hair back from her face and kiss her softly, trying to convey everything I feel for her.

She raises up on one elbow and looks down at me with a love in her eyes I never imagined knowing, much less deserving. "Wow," she says.

I grin, despite trying not to. "Yeah?"

"Yeah."

She kisses me then, and I swear I could make love to her again right now.

"You think parts ever wear out?" I ask, trying to refocus.

"Your parts?"

"Um-hm."

"I'm certainly not seeing any evidence of it," she says, smiling.

I push my hand through her hair; rub her jawline with my thumb. "I keep thinking we'll start to get enough of each other soon, and I'll stop waking you up at the crack of dawn."

"I like that you wake me up," she says, curving her leg across mine, her arm across my chest. "In fact, I keep thinking I'm going to wake up and none of this is going to be true."

"Me too," I admit.

"No way," she says, rubbing her thumb against my arm.

"Way."

"Guys like you don't have doubts like that."

"Yeah, we do. With girls like you."

"What like me?"

"Keepers."

"Why do you say that?"

"Because as ashamed as I am to admit it, you're the first woman I've ever been with that made me realize what this is really supposed to be about."

She kisses me softly and says, "I don't know what I did to deserve you, but thank you."

"And I don't know how I got lucky enough to find you."

We hold each other for a while, not saying anything, not needing to.

The birds have started to sing outside our bedroom window, a ray of sun slipping through the wooden blinds when I say, "There's something I've been thinking about."

"What?"

"We've been married six months, and I still haven't given you a honeymoon."

She lifts her head to look at me, smiling. "I could contest that."

"Okay, I didn't give you the whole thing."

"I don't need anything else, Thomas."

"Neither one of us wanted to leave Lexie after we first got married, but yesterday I mentioned to CeCe that I wanted to take you somewhere, and she said she and Holden would love to keep her while we take an official honeymoon."

Lila doesn't say anything for a few moments.

"I know how hard it is for you to think about leaving her, and I feel the same way. But CeCe and Holden would guard her with their lives."

"I know," she says finally. "That's really nice of them."

"They're crazy about Lexie."

"When?" she says, and I can tell she wants to say yes for me.

"We don't have to," I say. "I just think it would be good for us. Since we're not signing the new contract with the label, Holden thinks touring will be more important than ever. And the thought of being away from you and Lexie—"

"I know," she says, putting a finger to my lips. "Let's do it."

"Really?"

"Really. Are you going to tell me when and where?"

"Give me twenty-four hours."

"Okay."

"Meanwhile, back at the ranch," I say, sliding her under me again, my body making no secret of my intent.

"This ranch sure does have some frisky cowboys in its employ."

"We're known for it, ma'am," I say, and set out to prove her right.

♪

Lila

What If

IT'S THE NIGHT before Thomas and I are scheduled to leave for our honeymoon trip.

I'm excited about spending this time with him and looking forward to it, because I know it means a lot to him.

But sitting here on Lexie's bed with her tucked into the curve of my arm, I feel as if I am abandoning my child. Every what-if scenario I can imagine has run its trailer through my mind.

I'm reading her a book, and her eyes follow the colorful pages with riveted interest. I've explained to her where her daddy and I are going and when we'll be back, who she'll be staying with, how she'll get to school—everything I can think of to reassure her all is normal.

And she hasn't seemed the least bit anxious. Which should make me feel better, but it doesn't.

I lay the book down and lean away to look into her eyes. "Do you have any idea how much I'm going to miss you?"

She snuggles in tighter against me, and I hug her hard, tears streaming down my face even though I'm trying my best not to cry.

"CeCe and Holden have so many fun things planned for you. Brownie's going with you too, so he'll be able to play with Hank Junior and Patsy. You know how much he loves that. I'll be calling every day to check on you and hear about school and all that. We'll be gone for ten days, and then we'll be back. It'll seem like a blink."

Except I wonder if I believe my own words. I've never been away from Lexie for this long, and it kind of feels like I'm abandoning her. Logically, I know this isn't true. But I don't feel very logical at the moment.

The bedroom door opens, and Thomas walks in.

"How are my girls?" he asks.

I give him a teary smile and try to keep my voice from wavering. "All good here."

He comes over to sit on the other side of Lexie, putting his arm around us both. "You know I'm fine if you decide you don't want to go," he says.

"I know. We're good."

"We can Skype or FaceTime," he says. "That way we can put our eyes on our little girl every day."

"That's awesome," I say, and feel a little better at the thought.

"CeCe and Holden couldn't be any more excited about you staying with them while we're gone," he says, kissing the top of Lexie's head.

"It's all good," I say, reaching across to take his hand. And when he lifts it to his lips for a kiss, I can't help but worry that maybe it's all too good.

♪

Lila

Boundaries

WE'RE IN FIRST CLASS, and the flight attendant has been flirting with Thomas since take-off. Even with me sitting right next to him, and a wedding band on his left hand.

I'm not noting this out of jealousy. I'm used to the attention he gets from women, but as Macy's mom would say, "Child, have you no shame?"

The thought makes me smile, and gives me an idea for a lyric. I reach under the seat and pull my iPad from my bag, tapping an app and putting down some thoughts, then writing some actual lines.

Thomas leans over and looks at the screen, reading the words out loud.

> Girl, have you no shame
> Girl, are you so lame
> you don't see me sitting here
> you don't see me sitting here
> sitting right here, my dear

He groans and kisses my cheek. "I'm sorry, babe."

I smile at him. "Don't be. I might get a good song out of it."

"You're not jealous?"

"Why would I be jealous? You're not flirting back."

"True, but I've known some women who didn't have your knack for diplomacy."

"Would you rather I be jealous?" I ask, closing out the iPad screen.

"No, because it means you trust me."

"I do."

He takes my hand and laces his fingers through mine. "I miss her already," he says.

"I know. Me too."

"She's going to have a blast with CeCe and Holden."

"She might not want to come home."

He's quiet for a moment, and then, "Think we're like those helicopter parents you hear about?"

"If that means we're crazy in love with her and want the best for her, then I guess, yeah."

"I'm the big Black Hawk kind, chasing off all the bad guys. You're the little white kind like they use for hospitals, nurturing and—"

I smack his arm and laugh. "Maybe I'm the Black Hawk, and you're the little white—"

He cuts me off with tickling, and I'm laughing out loud when the flirty attendant walks by, giving me a severe look of disapproval. I let my gaze lock with hers, and we have a moment of acknowledgement between us. I think she finally gets it. He's mine.

♪

WE LAND IN Saint Martin around noon. The airport is nice and looks new. It sits close to the water, and the view coming in is breathtaking, the sea this incredible aqua green. Once we get through customs and collect our luggage, we meet the driver who is waiting for us just beyond the gate. He drives us the short distance to the port where the hotel has arranged for us to meet a private boat that will take us over to Anguilla. The driver of the boat is gracious and welcoming. We sit at the back on a white leather seat that's cushy and comfortable. The second mate offers us bottles of water or something stronger, if we prefer.

Thomas puts his arm around my shoulders, and sea spray spritzes our faces. The air feels warm and tropical, the sun a kiss on our shoulders. I look back at Saint Martin behind us, its deep green mountains a perfect backdrop to the sea. I snap a picture with my phone.

"So I Googled Anguilla," I say. "Want to hear what I learned?"

"Shoot," he says.

"Okay, it's something like sixteen miles long and three miles wide. The population is around 13,000. And they basically don't have any taxes on Anguilla."

"Whoa. I didn't know any such place existed."

"It's a British overseas territory. The coral reefs are supposed to be amazing. I would love to see them."

"We'll go snorkeling one day."

"I've never snorkeled."

"You'll love it. It's like stepping into another world."

"I can't wait."

The island ahead grows closer. "I knew it would be beautiful," I say, "but I had no idea it would be like this." I raise my phone and start taking some more pictures.

"It really is a paradise," Thomas says.

"It is."

"And we have ten whole days together here."

"I know," I say, hearing my own disbelief. I look over at him then, at the contentment in his expression and realize it mirrors my own. And again, as I have many times since the day we got married in a Nashville Baptist church, I have no idea how I ended up with this man.

♪

THE VICEROY HOTEL IS like something you would read about in a luxury vacation magazine. That's what Thomas has given me for a honeymoon, and I can't help but feel a little guilty. This five-star lifestyle is so far from anything I've ever known or deserve that I keep feeling as if I'm taking advantage or something.

The taxi that has driven us from the Anguilla port stops at the front entrance of the hotel. A smiling employee greets us and welcomes us to the island. A bellhop gets our luggage and directs us to the front desk.

The hotel lobby entrance is open. Doors aren't needed when you live in a climate like this. That seems amazing to me somehow. The floors leading to the front desk are marble with streaks of brown, cream, and gold. Just past the check-in desk is another opening like the one at the front. From here, you can see straight out to an infinity pool and the sea beyond.

Once we're checked in, the bellhop walks us to our room. The hotel property is a wide expanse of marble and tile. We pass another pool, and there is a low Caribbean beat playing around the bar.

The bell boy places our luggage in the large walk-in closet, leaving us with a quiet nod.

I look around the suite, finding it hard to process. There is an enormous living area with a sink and a refrigerator. The bedroom is the most luxurious thing I've ever seen, a sprawling king-size bed in the middle. The bathroom includes a tub big enough for four people and a shower that is equally big. I glance at Thomas, not knowing what to say.

"Do you not like it?" he asks, sounding worried.

"What? Yes, of course," I say. "It's incredible. I don't think I realized places like this existed outside of movies."

"Not what you were expecting?" he asks, as if he thinks he's disappointed me.

"Thomas. It's amazing. I just don't feel like I deserve—"

"I know," he says, walking closer to run his hand through my hair. "But you do. Anything that I have is yours. And this is our honeymoon. Let's enjoy every minute of it."

I start to say something, but don't want to sound ungrateful, so I take his hand and pull him to the open doors that lead onto the balcony, facing the ocean. The beach stretches out before us, a white ribbon of sand that meets and melds with its blue-green sea. "It could not be more beautiful," I say. "Thank you for bringing me here."

He slips his hands around my waist and lifts me up against him, kissing me and then letting me slide back down his body. "Think we ought to christen the room before we take a swim?"

"Aren't you supposed to do that with Champagne?"

"Or anything bubbly. I can be bubbly."

"All right, then," I say, smiling at him.

He leans in and scoops me up in his arms, walking back into the room, and with one booted foot, closes the door behind us.

♪

Thomas

Waves

SO I COULD get used to this. Fast.

The sun has dropped in the sky with the onset of late afternoon. I'm lazing in a lounge chair with an ice bucket set up beside me, a cold bottle of Champagne and two glasses.

Lila is floating in the shallow water not far from the sand's edge, the gentle waves lifting her body up, then dipping down in a gentle rhythm. I've done my share of scoffing at guys who were clearly whipped, so I know how corny it sounds. But I could watch her forever. I never want to stop looking at her. Or for that matter, touching her. Holding her. Making love to her.

She flips like a dolphin, from her back to her stomach, now swimming with long, beautiful strokes just behind the breaking waves.

My phone buzzes, and I pull it from the bag under my chair, glancing at the screen. It's a text from Holden.

Any trouble in paradise?
Not unless perfection is trouble.
Island beautiful?
Incredible. How's Lexie?
CeCe just picked her up from school. Had a play session with the dogs in the back yard.
I know she loved that.
She's got the cutest darn giggle.
I know. You better watch out.
What?
You're gonna be wanting one of your own.
Agree. Enjoy. Putting you to work when you get back.

I'm thinking we might come home and get Lexie and just move here.

Hell, no.

I laugh and take a picture of Lila swimming in the ocean, then send it to him.

Y'all can swim in Nashville.

Not quite the same.

You know you love it here.

Yeah, I do. I promise not to run away.

Good. Later.

Later.

Lila is still swimming. I pull off my T-shirt and walk out to join her so I can give her an update on Lexie.

She looks up and spots me coming; she's waving and smiling. I stop for a moment just so I can freeze-frame her beauty, be able to bring it up in my mind when we're not together.

She waves me toward her. I smile and run to meet her.

♪

Lila

How to Save a Life

WE SPEND THE first couple of days on the island in a sort of haze. That's the only word I can think of to describe the utter luxury of putting nothing on our daily schedule except each other and whatever it is that we want to do together.

Every night, right before I go to sleep, and right as I'm waking up in the morning, I feel as if I'm encircled in a haze of happiness. I feel guilty for being so happy. It's not that I don't miss my Lexie. I do. With a deep ache. But I realize the importance of having this time with Thomas and how I should cherish every minute of it. We FaceTime with Lexie a couple of times a day, and I can see that she is happy and having a wonderful time with CeCe and Holden.

In the mornings, I write. I finish the song I started on the plane, and it ends up being pretty good. I record the melody with an app on my phone, and Thomas walks out onto our terrace just as I'm finishing. He's just gotten out of the shower. A towel is anchored at his waist, and he has another around his shoulders, using one end to dry his hair. My gaze settles on the curve and angle of his bicep. I wonder if I will ever look at him without this immediate surge of wanting.

"That sounds great," he says.

"The lyric turned out pretty cute," I say.

"Yeah. But I mean your voice."

"Thanks," I say.

"How long are you going to avoid the subject?"

"What subject?"

"You singing."

"Don't you think one in the family is enough?"

"Not when it means ignoring talent like yours."

I meet his gaze and say, "That means more to me than you can know, but I think I've received more than my share of good fortune."

"Sweetie, you deserve everything you have." He sits down in the chair next to mine, and runs his hand across the back of my hair. "You don't talk about it, but I know you don't think you do."

"How could anyone deserve everything I've been given? I have a child I would give my life for, and you—"

"And you don't think you should ask for more?"

I shrug, looking out at the ocean, and then say honestly, "No. I don't."

"You were given an incredible talent, Lila. You don't need to pay for what you have by not using it."

Put like that, I guess it does sound unreasonable. But when you've seen a side of life that is so very different from what I have now, you get a little worried that your once-proven-correct theory of "nothing lasts forever" might prove itself true again.

"It scares me, I guess."

"What does?"

"Taking risks with what I have."

"Lila," he says, reaching out to touch the side of my face. "I love you. All of you. And your writing and singing is part of who you are. It's something you have a right to express. If you want to, I want you to. Since we got married, you stopped singing for demos. I know you're writing, but you won't let us consider using any of your songs."

"That would be cheating."

"How do you figure?"

"Because it would be obvious why you chose my song. You know y'all can have your pick of pretty much anything written in Nashville. And by the top writers."

"If we used one of your songs, it would be because we thought it was right for us."

"That's what you would tell yourself," I say.

"You're a tough sell, you know it?"

"Thomas, I love you for caring. I just plain love you. And it's enough."

"But it might not be one day," he says, with a new worry in his voice.

"How about if I promise to let you know if it's not?"

He's quiet for a long string of moments before saying, "Can I ask you something?"

"Anything."

"Do you worry about us and what we have because of your dad and your mom?"

I could make light of the question, not give it the weight he's allotting it, but I owe him honesty. And so I say, "They were crazy about each other at one time. Or at least that's what I remember Mama telling me when I was a little girl."

"And what happened?"

I shake my head. "I don't really know. My dad drank, and he just started to change. He got really jealous, and it was like my mom couldn't do anything right. There were some really horrible fights."

Thomas takes my hand, links our fingers together. "Baby, I'm so sorry."

"Sometimes, I wonder why she didn't leave. Why she didn't just go somewhere and start a new life with me. It seems easy from where I am now. But I guess it's not."

I consider what she's said for a moment before saying, "My uncle is a prosecuting attorney in Georgia. He used to take me to football games when I was growing up, and after I got older, I liked to ask him about his work. I knew he had met a lot of bad guys. But I remember him saying this one thing. That so many of the men he ended up sending to prison had good in them. They let themselves become eaten up with some toxic emotion like jealousy or envy, and they committed a single act that resulted in the permanent loss of their freedom. I guess the part I always found so sad was that every one of them had a moment when they could have chosen not to do what they were going to do."

Tears well in my eyes and slide down my cheeks. I wipe them away with the back of my hand, and, seeing me, Thomas makes a low sound of pain and reaches for me, pulling me out of my chair and onto his lap. He holds me with such love and such compassion that I can't hold back the sobs welling up from some deep place. I wrap my arms around his neck and bury my face against him, just letting myself grieve.

I don't know how long we sit there like that, me crying, him holding me. But I do know I have never let myself mourn this way.

In doing so now, I realize that maybe, just maybe, it will be the first step I've ever taken toward healing. And in this, he has given me yet another gift.

♪

Thomas

The Millionaire and His Wife

ON THE FOURTH day of our trip, we decide to take a day excursion to a deserted island close to Saint Martin that is supposed to be incredibly beautiful.

I've been worried about Lila since the morning she broke down and cried with the mourning of a completely broken heart. I've never felt so helpless in my life. But I realized at some point while I was holding her shaking body in my arms that she needed to mourn. And I was grateful she felt safe enough to do it with me.

All day yesterday, she was sad and quiet. And I just let her be what she needed to be. We hung out at the pool, reading and listening to music. I can't exactly explain it, but this island feels like a place where you can absorb things that need to be absorbed.

When she woke me this morning with a sweet kiss and a thank you, I could see in her eyes that some of the darkness had lifted. A day spent in the sun on a beautiful island seemed like a place to go from there.

And so, along with eight other couples and a family, we board the hotel's plush cruiser at just after nine o'clock, heading away from Anguilla on a smooth sea. It only takes about twenty minutes to reach the island, and some of the other guests cheer when it comes into sight.

"It's beautiful," Lila says, pointing her camera lens at the small jewel of land set in the sea before us. She snaps pictures from different angles, then turns the camera on me and follows me with it even when I duck.

"I'm not the view here," I say, reaching out to grab it.

"Bet I could sell these online for quite a bit," she teases.

"I think I have a few of you I could sell for more," I say, pulling her to me and whispering in her ear the exact photography session I'm talking about.

She laughs softly and says, "You win."

I put my arms around her, and we lean against the side of the boat, looking out at the glittering ocean water.

"This place is almost unreal," Lila says.

"Next time we'll bring Lexie," I say.

"Could we?" she asks, tilting her head back to look up at me.

"Sure, we could."

"She would love it," Lila says.

A woman in a bikini walks over and leans against the railing next to us. She has long black hair and a face that barely conceals evidence of some early plastic surgery. "Excuse me," she says. "Are you Thomas Franklin?"

I reach for my politest tone, even though her question feels like an intrusion on my time with Lila. I know I don't have a right to resent it, but here, on our honeymoon, I do. "I am," I say, giving her a less-than-encouraging smile.

"Oh, my goodness," she says. "I'm Tena Carson, and I told my husband you were! I can't believe you're here on this boat!"

"My wife and I are on our honeymoon," I say with a polite nod, hoping she will take the hint.

"It's a beautiful place, isn't it?" Lila says, taking the gracious route.

"It is. And aren't you the lucky one getting to see it with him?"

"I am," Lila agrees.

"You and your husband enjoy the day, ma'am," I say, again hoping she'll take the hint.

"Well, you too," she says, backing away with a barely concealed look of insult.

Once she's gone, Lila says, "You didn't have to do that for me."

"I didn't mean to be an ass. I just want our time here to be about us."

"I know, but you probably just lost a fan."

"I'm not going to worry about that right now," I say, ducking my head to kiss the side of her neck.

A few minutes later, we're close in to the island, a small paradise of land rimmed in white sand, deep green vegetation rising up behind the beach. The captain anchors the boat close enough that we can swim in if we choose to, and Lila and I do. The crew takes some of the passengers in with dinghies and then goes back for food and beverages which they set up under colorful umbrellas on the strip of white sand.

We swim and float for a bit because the water feels so good and then stretch out on towels to absorb the warm rays of the sun. The woman from the boat walks by and makes a noticeable effort to ignore us. I feel a little guilty about my attitude from earlier, but I don't think she's going to let me make up for it. At one point, I glance up and find her taking pictures of us from several yards away. She immediately lowers the camera although she keeps her gaze even with mine, as if letting me know she's found a way to pay me back.

I could get up and go ask her to delete the pictures, but what's the point? If it makes her feel better to sell them to some tabloid, she should have at it.

Lila lifts her head then, and says, "What is it?"

"Nothing," I say, standing and then reaching out for her hand. "Why don't we take a hike around the island?"

"Sounds great," she says.

I double-check with a crew member about what time the boat will leave the island, and we then walk inland.

There are paths already cut through the dense greenery, most likely forged by other day tourists. We pick one to follow and walk to a soundtrack of birds, whose tunes I don't recognize but find beautiful all the same.

"I feel like we're on Gilligan's Island," Lila says, looking over her shoulder with a laugh.

"You watched that show?"

"You didn't?"

"Well, yeah, I did, but I wouldn't have pictured you as a fan."

"I LOVE Gilligan's Island."

"So who would we be?"

"Definitely not Gilligan and the captain."

"Or the professor and Mary Ann. Or Ginger."

"That leaves Mr. and Mrs. Howell."

"He's a little stuffed-shirt for me," I say.

"But they're married. And Thurston would do anything for Lovey. Makes him a stand-up guy in my opinion."

I catch up with her and snag an arm around her waist, lifting her off the ground. "So maybe I'm Thurston."

"Except better-looking," she says, giggling.

"Well, thank goodness for that."

We've been walking for about thirty minutes when we reach the other side of the island. The vegetation gives way to a rocky shoreline, completely different from the white sandy beach we anchored off earlier.

The incline to the water is fairly steep. "Maybe we shouldn't go any farther," I say, taking Lila's hand.

"Let's go see," she says. "It's not far."

I give in to her tugging, and we make our way slowly down the incline to the testy waves below. We find a large rock to sit on, facing the ocean, while the water snaps and snarls at its base.

"It's like we're the only two people on Earth," Lila says. "It feels so isolated here."

"There aren't too many places that feel like that anymore," I agree.

"No," she says. "There are a lot of positives about how connected our world is today. But sometimes, it would be nice to fully disconnect. In our regular lives, that seems less and less possible."

"I have an idea," I say.

"What?"

"When we get home, why don't we pick one day a week where we do exactly that? All phones off. Computers. TV. Radio. The whole thing."

"You would do that?" she asks, tipping her head back to look at me.

"I actually think it would be good for all of us. Lexie, too, because our focus on her wouldn't be diluted by the constant reminders of what's going on outside our house."

"I love that idea," she says.

"Cool. We'll do it."

A clap of thunder sounds behind us. We both look back to the other side of the island where dark storm clouds have turned the sky from light blue to a deep, angry gray.

"Uh-oh," I say. "We better get back."

We climb the rocks to the path. When we reach the top of the steep incline, Lila stops for a moment, and leans over with her hands on her knees.

"You okay?" I ask.

"Just catching my breath," she says. "Go on. I'll be right there."

"You're good," I say.

She draws in a few deep breaths, prompting me to ask, "Are you sure you're all right?"

She smiles and nods. "Yep. Let's go."

We head back at a fast walk, but halfway there, the rain begins to fall, large pelting drops that sting our skin and plaster our hair to our heads. I'm leading the way, holding onto Lila's hand, when she pulls at me and says, "Can we go a little slower?"

Surprised, I check my pace, wondering if something is wrong. Then I think about the fact that we haven't been using birth control, and the thought that she could be pregnant strikes me in the heart.

"Are you sure you're all right?" I ask.

"Yes," she says, "just a little tired."

I put my hand on her face and look into her eyes, my heart pounding hard. "Any chance we could be making a baby?"

A smile breaks across her mouth, and she leans against the trunk of a palm tree. "I don't think so, but would you be okay with it if we were?"

"More than okay," I say. "Like ecstatic okay."

"I love you," she says, drawing in a deep breath.

"Not as much as I love you," I say, and then, bending my knees, add, "Piggyback ride for you."

"It's too far for you to carry me," she protests.

"Are you insulting my manhood, woman?"

"I would never—" she begins with a giggle.

"Then all aboard," I command.

She gets on with notable reluctance, and I take off at a jog, bouncing her along like a child on her first pony.

It's raining even harder when we reach the beach, sheets of it that ping like needles. It takes me a moment to realize that all the umbrellas are gone, the food packed up.

There's not a person in sight.

And for that matter, no boat either.

♪

Lila

Under a Tree on an Island

"DID THEY REALLY leave us?" I ask, hearing the disbelief in my own voice.

Lightning cracks across the sky, striking the ocean surface before us.

Thomas shakes his head and says, "I don't know how that could be possible. Even my backpack with our phones in it is gone."

"They'll come back," I say. "Surely, someone will miss us."

"Eventually."

The rain is pouring even more now; rain like I've never seen before. Thomas takes my hand and pulls me back across the beach to the path that led us to the other side of the island.

"We need to find some shelter until they do come back," he says, raising his voice above the wind now whipping sand against our ankles.

I stumble once, and he catches me before I fall. I hurry to keep up with him, but find myself struggling again. I make a resolution to get back to working out on a daily basis. And then I wonder if I actually could be pregnant. I remember how tired I was before I realized I was pregnant with Lexie. A flare of excitement lights up inside me, followed by an instant flash of worry.

I think about the first few months after Lexie was born, and how I hadn't known for sure that she would make it. Could that happen again?

I stop my runaway thoughts right there. Thomas finds us a spot that is semi-protected from the rain, a canopy of trees that have grown into a tangle at the top, as if the trees were each struggling to maintain their connection with the sunlight. We sit down at the base of one, our backs against the trunk. He wraps his arms around me, and I snuggle up to him.

"Are you worried?" I ask, raising my voice above the still churning wind.

"About someone coming back?"

"Yes."

"No, at the very least, that same boat comes to the island every day with new passengers. Even if they don't miss us, they'll be bringing in fresh victims."

My laugh comes out as a snort. "How bad can it be? A night with you on a deserted island? No one else around for miles?"

He smiles down at me, raising his eyebrow in wicked suggestion. "It could make for a memorable experience."

"Living a fantasy and all that," I agree. "Did you ever see that movie with Madonna where she's stranded on an island with a fisherman she can't stand?"

"I don't think so," Thomas says.

"By the time they get off the island, she's crazy about him."

"What happens when they get back to the real world?"

"Misunderstandings abound, and they don't end up together."

"That sucks."

"Yeah, I wanted the happy ending."

"You mean the one like we have," he says, leaning in to kiss my neck.

"That one," I say, lifting my face to his. I kiss him then with all the love I feel for him. I don't bother to censor it anymore. At first, I was afraid to let him see the extent of my feelings. I knew how vulnerable it made me. But at some point, I realized I wanted to give him everything. All of me. No holding back. So I do. And we make love in the rain.

♪

WHEN THE LAST of the storm disappears out to sea, darkness has settled over the island. Now that the wind is no longer roaring around us, the quiet feels almost eerie.

Thomas stands and takes my hand. "Let's make us a spot on the beach."

We're both soaked, and I'm starting to shiver.

"Come on," he says, "we need to warm you up."

I follow him to the beach. The Moon has crept up over the horizon, full and bright as if it holds no grudge against the storm that earlier eclipsed it.

"Let's go for a swim," Thomas says. "The ocean will warm us up."

"But we'll just be wetter," I say, less than thrilled by the thought.

"Trust me," he says, pulling off his T-shirt and then his swimming trunks.

"Naked in the moonlight," I say. "How can I resist?"

"Hey, there's a good hook for you. You can write that song when we get back."

I laugh and also shimmy out of my clothes as well. He gives me a long look, and I know he's thinking of other ways to warm me up again. He makes a groaning sound, and then swoops me in his arms, walking with determination to the water's edge and then farther in until we're both up to our shoulders.

And he's right, of course. The ocean is like a warm bath, gently lapping around us with no memory at all of its earlier angry churning, as if it's determined to earn our forgiveness.

♪

Thomas

Dissed

THE BOAT APPEARS on the horizon at mid-morning, same as our arrival yesterday.

I wish I could capture the look on the captain's face when he spots Lila and me standing on the beach. He brings the dinghy in to meet us, and it's immediately obvious no one even realized we were missing.

The captain gets out of the small boat and runs to us, water splashing up on his white shorts. "What has happened? You were here all night?" he asks, panic in his voice.

"Yes," I say. "We seemed to have missed our ride when the storm came up."

He shakes his head in confusion. Tears actually spring to his eyes and start down his face. "We did a count, and everyone was present. We were hurrying because of the storm, but—"

"Who did the count?" I ask.

"The woman with black hair. Mrs. Carson."

I raise a hand to stop him, glancing at Lila, who clearly can't believe it. "I guess I lost that fan," I say.

"Are you saying she lied deliberately about you being on the boat?" the captain asks, wide-eyed.

"It doesn't matter now," I say. "Can you just give us a ride back to Anguilla?"

"Oh, absolutely, sir. I am so sorry. I cannot believe this has happened."

"It's all good," I say, not wanting to make him feel any worse. But it's clear that he does, and he goes out of his way to try to make up for it. At one point, I tell him, "Please. Don't worry about it. Nothing bad came of it. We're not going to complain to the hotel or anything like that."

The gratitude in his eyes is a little humbling. I suspect his livelihood depends on this excursion, and I guess I can understand his concern.

Within thirty minutes, the hotel's private boat arrives to pick us up, a tray of coffee and incredible-smelling bread waiting for us in the cabin.

Lila and I tackle both, as if we haven't eaten in days instead of the twenty-four hours it's been.

"Something about not having access to food puts you in starvation mode, doesn't it?" I say, deciding then that this is the best coffee I've ever had and definitely the best bread.

Lila takes a bite of her roll. "I still can't believe that woman would intentionally do that."

"Yeah. I guess I'm starting to reach the point where not much surprises me."

"The price of fame?"

"I guess. Who knew?"

"I hope for her sake, we don't run into her again."

"I hope for her sake, we don't either," I say.

♪

WHEN WE GET to the hotel, a full breakfast is waiting in our room, along with flowers and a note of sincere apology from the management. Someone had turned our backpacks and our phones in to Lost and Found, and those have been left neatly on the bed.

"In today's world," Lila says, pouring herself a glass of orange juice, "I'm sure they expect to be sued."

"It wasn't their fault," I say. "But I guess some people do look for an opportunity."

We eat until we're stuffed, and then make a FaceTime call home. Lexie is already in school, but CeCe assures us everything is fine, although they had gotten a little concerned when we didn't call last night. I tell her everything that happened, and she thinks I'm kidding at first.

"All because you dissed a fan?" she says.

"Apparently," I say. "And I didn't really diss her. I just wanted to enjoy my honeymoon with my wife."

"Psycho-B," CeCe says, anger underscoring the word.

I laugh then because the language is so un-CeCe.

"Are you both okay?" she asks.

Lila assures her that we are and promises we'll call back in the afternoon when Lexie is out of school.

Once we hang up, Lila heads for the shower, and I join her a few minutes later. We're both so tired that for the first time since we've been married, we don't do anything except get clean. We towel ourselves dry and slide into the luxurious hotel bed, wrapping our arms around each other and almost instantly falling asleep.

♪

Lila

To Leave a Place

WE SLEEP UNTIL dinner.

The blackout curtains in the room must have convinced our bodies that it was nighttime. Or we were just that tired.

I hear the shower running and realize Thomas has already gotten up. I stretch an arm across the bed, deciding to join him. I slide off the mattress, but just as I stand, a wave of dizziness hits me so hard that I stumble and fall onto the nightstand.

My shoulder bumps the lamp and knocks it to the floor. I hear the shower turn off, and not wanting Thomas to find me like this, I slip back into bed, willing the dizziness to stop.

The bathroom door opens, and Thomas's footsteps sound quietly on the marble floor, as if he's trying not to wake me.

"Hey," I say, just as he reaches the side of the bed.

"Hey, yourself, sleepyhead." He turns on the lamp next to him, and then spotting the one on the floor next to my side of the bed, he says, "What happened?"

"I—I started to get up and got a little dizzy. I probably just need to eat something."

He immediately comes over and sits down beside me, looking at me with worry-filled eyes. "Are you okay?"

"Yeah, I think so."

"Are you hungry?"

"A little, maybe."

"Do you feel like going out for dinner, or we could just do room service?"

"Would you mind if we do the room service?"

"Course not," he says. He looks at me for several long seconds, as if trying to decide whether or not I'm keeping anything from him. "Think maybe we ought to pick up a pregnancy test tomorrow?"

"It might not be a bad idea," I say. "I'm actually starting to wonder myself. Although I've definitely gotten dizzy before when I've gone too long without eating. It's probably the food thing. No big deal."

"How about I run you a bath and order us some dinner?"

"That sounds wonderful."

"Then we'll call Lexie?"

"Perfect," I say.

♪

I WAKE UP the next morning, surprised to see that it's after ten o'clock. I never sleep this late. I flick on the lamp and find a note from Thomas on the pillow. He's gone out for a run.

I get up, take a quick shower, relieved to find the dizziness gone this morning. I order some coffee, and drink it on the terrace where the light ocean breeze feels heavenly. I think about everything that's happened the last couple of days and realize I hadn't liked the feeling of being trapped on that island. Maybe it's my tendency to feel claustrophobic in tight places, but I like knowing I can leave a place when I want to.

And that makes me think of my dad. The cell he sits in twenty-three hours out of every twenty-four in a Virginia prison.

I don't know how he stands it.

It's not often that I let myself think about him. There's nothing to be gained by doing so. Nothing I can change. It's never been easy for me to merge in my head the two people I have known as my father. The one before. And the one after.

I take another sip of my coffee and stare out at the ocean horizon, wondering if he regrets what he did. If he would take it back if he could.

Somehow, I think he would. I remember the good side of my father. The one I saw mostly when I was a little girl. Before jealousy and possessiveness took the reins of his relationship with my mother. It's hard to imagine that they might have once felt for each other what Thomas and I feel for each other. But then, most relationships start out as wonderful.

What happens to trigger the darkness? Eclipse all the good?

I feel a little flutter of panic at the questions. Because who's to say Thomas and I will be different in the end? Is it arrogant to think that kind of erosion could never happen in our marriage? Is it possible that I could start to feel jealous of the attention he gets from women because of his career?

I set my cup on the table in front of me, noticing that my hand is shaking.

I hear the door to our room open, then swing shut.

Thomas calls out, "You up, babe?"

"Here," I say.

He walks out to the terrace and leans in to kiss me on the cheek.

"Hey, sleepy girl," he says.

"I know. What's up with that? I'm usually awake with the dawn. Want some coffee?" I ask, waving a hand at the silver tray service.

"I'd love some," he says. "Let me get out of these icky clothes."

He's back in a couple of minutes, and I pour him a cup.

"So what are we doing today?" I ask.

"Not getting stranded on a desert island," he says.

I smile a little. "I'm glad our ride came. But you have to admit, in hindsight it's a little funny."

"I'm not there yet," he says, taking a sip of his coffee.

"It could have been a lot worse."

"Yeah, I guess that's true."

"Actually, I wouldn't want to repeat the experience," I say. "Being trapped there made me think about my dad."

Thomas looks up, clearly surprised by my admission. "Yeah?"

"Just the whole never-being-able-to-leave-a-place thing."

"It's an awful thought."

I sigh and try to force a light note in my voice when I say, "He put himself there."

Thomas is quiet for a moment, before saying, "If you ever want to go see him, Lila, I'll go with you."

"I don't," I say, a sharp note in my voice. "I'm sorry," I add instantly. "Thank you. But I don't ever want to see him there."

Thomas takes my hand and pulls me up from my chair and into his arms. He holds me tight against him, and I press my cheek to his chest, loving the strong beat of his heart. I know he wants to absorb my grief, carry it for me. And the realization of that makes me love him so much that it hurts.

♪

Thomas

Like Grace

WE'RE ON THE BEACH later that afternoon, stretched out on the comfortable chairs provided by the hotel. Lila is lying on her stomach, chin on her folded arms, her eyes not visible to me behind dark sunglasses.

"Are you disappointed?" I ask.

She turns to look at me then, the glasses still in place. "About the pregnancy test?"

"Yeah," I say, trying to sound nonchalant about it.

"Maybe a little," she says.

"I know we haven't really talked about it too much one way or the other, but I guess maybe the idea had taken hold, at least a little bit anyway."

"You would have been excited about it?"

"Of course," I say. "Would you?"

She nods once and admits, "Because of everything that happened with Lexie, I'd be a little scared too. But if she's shown me anything, it's that perfect isn't always what we think it is."

"Do you want to start trying?"

She smiles at me. "I'm not sure it's physically possible for us to 'try' more times a day than we already are."

I laugh, thump her arm with a finger. "I mean targeted trying."

"Oh," she says. "Targeted trying."

We both laugh then, and she slides her glasses down to look at me. No one has ever looked at me the way Lila does. No one has ever made me feel the way she makes me feel. As if I was put here on this Earth to be an extension of her and for her to be an extension of me. It's the most incredible feeling I've ever had in my life. A gift I know I've never done anything to deserve. Maybe that's what makes it all the more meaningful. Like grace, I guess. It's not something we earn. It's

39

just something we're given. I vow then and there, taking in the face of my beautiful wife, to do my best to be deserving of it.

♪

Lila

What It Is

THE FIRST COUPLE of weeks after we get home from Anguilla are incredibly busy.

It feels a little funny at first, reentering the orbit of our normal lives after ten days of nothing to do but soak up each other. For the first few days, Thomas and I spend most of our time with Lexie. She's clingy at first, and it's clear how much she missed us, despite all the fun she had at CeCe and Holden's house. It actually feels good to know that we were missed.

I'm now taking her for physical therapy appointments at Vanderbilt on Monday, Wednesday, and Friday. The sessions really seem to be helping with her muscle strength. Every afternoon, she throws the ball for Brownie in the backyard. I've noticed that the distance has increased so that Brownie has to run farther each time. I'm not sure who enjoys it more. Him or her. But by the time they're done, she's giggling, and he's panting hard with a big, gooberish smile on his face.

Thomas and Holden have spent a good bit of time planning the upcoming tour. They've invested in a bus, which is like a luxurious house on wheels. They've also been working on new songs. Thomas tells CeCe about the song I wrote on our honeymoon: Boundaries. She calls one afternoon when I'm on the way to pick up Lexie from school to ask if she can hear it.

"CeCe," I say. "Don't feel like you need to listen to it. It's probably not up to—"

"Can I be the judge of that?" CeCe interrupts in a kind voice. "I know you're writing some great stuff, Lila. And if you're not going to sing it yourself, I'd love a shot at it. From what Thomas says, it sounds like something that would really fit in with the songs we're working on now."

"Seriously?"

"Girl, when are you going to let yourself believe that you have the goods?"

"Thank you," I say. "It's just—I don't want to ask for anything more. I already have so much."

"Lila, I don't believe God gives us any talents He doesn't want us to use. Using yours doesn't mean you're asking for anything more in this life."

"Somehow to me, it does," I admit.

"I know," she says. "And I get it. But guilt is a negative prison we put ourselves in. And there's nothing to be accomplished from it or gained by it. We use what we have to try to make this world a better place in whatever way possible. That's a positive thing."

I've just turned in to the school parking lot when I say, "Thank you, CeCe. And yes, I'd love to play you the song. All I have is the melody and lyric. We haven't put any music to it."

"Can you email me what you have?"

"Sure, as soon as I get home with Lexie."

"Okay," CeCe says, and I hear the smile in her voice. "Give sweet girl a smile for me," she adds.

"I will," I say, sitting for a few moments after we end the call, just thinking.

Maybe it's time I actually let myself start to believe what CeCe just said to me. It's true that I can look at my love for music and desire to express it in two different ways. The first being as a means for getting more out of this world, recognition, money. And the second as a way to give back for all that I have been given.

I know in my heart that this is truly what it means to me. And the only reason I need for letting what I create out into the world. I don't want the recognition, and in this life I now lead, I certainly don't want to do it for the money.

Whatever I have to give, I'm not going to hide it anymore. Or immediately discount it as insignificant. It is what it is. And I am who I am. I think it really is time for me to let that be enough.

♪

Thomas

Ruined

WE PLANNED FOR the tour to be a month long.

I used to get excited about the idea of going on the road. Seeing new faces and meeting new people. Now, just the thought of it makes me feel nearly ill.

On the night before the morning we're scheduled to leave, Lila and I are lying in bed, holding each other with the awareness that we're going to be apart for almost a month before we see each other again. We've just completed one of our targeted "trying" sessions, as we both now call it. I lean over to kiss her shoulder. "I don't think I can stand to be away from you," I say.

"I wish we could come with you," Lila says. "But with Lexie's school—"

"I know. Maybe next time we can plan to take her out for a while and bring along a tutor."

"I would love that," Lila says.

"So it's not really that long," I say, trying to convince myself. "I'll fly back in twenty-four days—"

"—eight hours, fifteen minutes, and thirty-four seconds," Lila finishes.

I groan a little.

"It's okay," she says. "You know how fast the days go by. Y'all will be so busy with the tour that it won't seem like it's that long."

I nod, but I know that it will, and that every minute I'm apart from them will be torture. "You'll have plenty to do," I say. "You know my mom's coming in next weekend. She can't wait to see you and Lexie."

"I'm going to plan some fun stuff for us to do," Lila says.

"She's more excited about seeing you two than she is about seeing me, when the tour is in Atlanta."

"I think that's more about Lexie than it is about me."

"Neither one of us can compete with her."

Lila smiles and rubs her hand across my chest. We're quiet for a few moments, and then I force myself to say something I've been wanting to say. "I know we haven't been apart like this yet. And there's something I just need for you to hear."

"What?" she asks softly.

"You don't need to worry about me even looking at another woman, Lila. If the situation were reversed, with you leaving and me staying here, I think I would be worried."

"You shouldn't be. You've ruined me for any other man."

I pull her tight into the circle of my arms. "That works both ways you know."

She leans back to look at me with a smile. "I've ruined you for any other man?" She starts to giggle then, and I roll her over onto her back.

"Come here, you," I say, kissing her neck and making my way down her body.

"Are you good for one more trying session?"

"You know it, baby."

♪

Lila

Not So Quickly

IT DOESN'T TAKE long for me to realize my claims of time passing quickly are just so much false assurance.

I'm busy enough throughout the day so that Thomas being gone is tolerable, but the nights are a different story altogether. Brownie sleeps in the bed next to me. And even though I try to keep my tears silent, he somehow knows immediately and scoots closer to lick my cheek, comforting me.

It's not as if Thomas and I don't talk and text throughout the day, but it's not the same. I put on my most cheerful disposition for our conversations. I don't want him worrying about us, and the truth is I know I would have to say almost nothing for him to end the tour and come back. And that wouldn't be fair to CeCe and Holden.

So I put a calendar page on the refrigerator, and every morning, Lexie and I cross off a day. I point to the date when Daddy will be home, reminding her that it's not long at all.

Mrs. Franklin arrives on that first Friday. It's really good to see her. So many things about her remind me of Thomas. And Lexie lights up the minute she walks in the room. We spend some time shopping on Saturday at Whole Foods, and that night, Mrs. Franklin fixes us a southern meal to rival all southern meals: mashed potatoes, biscuits, lima beans, and peach cobbler for dessert.

We're in the living room having the cobbler with some coffee when she looks at me and says, "I'd like to thank you, Lila."

"For what?" I ask, surprised.

"For being such a blessing to my son. You've anchored him. Centered him. I used to worry so much about him in this life and all the temptations that come with it. But I don't worry anymore because I see who he lives for. You and precious Lexie. Those old temptations have no sway over him now, and I actually go to sleep at night without any of my old worries."

"Thank you, Mrs. Franklin," I say, feeling a little overwhelmed by her sincerity. "For everything you just said. To be honest with you, I'm not sure how any of this happened. But I love him."

"I know you do," Mrs. Franklin interrupts softly. "For a woman like you to love my son. Well, that's all a mother can hope for."

I feel the tears well in my eyes, and, to my embarrassment, they slide down my cheeks unchecked. "Can I be honest with you about something?"

"Of course you can, dear."

"Sometimes," I say, "I think it's all too good to be true."

"I've felt that way at times in my life," she says. "Maybe we all do, when it feels like we have more than we deserve. For me, it makes me more determined to be grateful for what I have. And to just do my best to show that in the way I live."

She reaches across to take my hand and squeezes hard.

"I'm really glad you're here," I say.

"Me, too, sweetie," she says.

♪

Lila

Trap Doors

WHEN I WAKE up the next morning, with Brownie beside me, the room is still dark. I glance at the clock and see that it's not yet six.

I have this instant feeling of something not being right. It's only then that I realize my breathing feels different.

I try to pull in a deep breath, but it feels incomplete, as if I can't draw it from its normal place. I try again with the same result. A feeling of panic starts to wash over me, and I force myself to be calm. I sit up and swing my legs over the side of the bed, feeling instantly dizzy.

I've had a moment or two of this since those episodes on our honeymoon, but nothing that felt alarming. This shortness of breath, I've never had before. I start to stand, but the room tilts, and I immediately drop onto the bed.

I lie flat on my back, staring up at the ceiling, trying to pull in air and starting to panic, which is only making my breathing worse.

Brownie whines as if to ask me what's wrong. I rub his head in reassurance.

I close my eyes and reach for calm, trying to put my mind in a peaceful place. I instantly picture the beach in Anguilla where Thomas and I walked every morning, try to feel the lap of the water against my ankles, the warmth of the morning sun on my shoulders, the quiet roar of the ocean waves in my ears.

I strive for a deeper breath then and feel a bit more air filling my lungs. The panicky feeling starts to subside a bit.

A half hour or so passes before I finally feel like trying to get up again. The dizziness is now gone. I make my way to the bathroom and take a shower, leaning against the marble wall the entire time.

I don't think I'm pregnant but decide to pick up a test for later.

After I get dressed, I walk carefully to the kitchen, feeling a small wave or two of dizziness. Then I'm fine again, as I let Brownie out in the back yard and make some coffee. I pull two cups from the cabinet for Mrs. Franklin and me. I hear her bedroom door open just as the kettle on the stove starts to whistle, and I pour the hot water into a French press pot.

"Good morning," she says, walking into the kitchen with a yawn.

"Good morning," I say. "How did you sleep?"

"Wonderful. And you?"

"Good." I decide not to mention the episode.

"Our Lexie still in bed?"

"I was just getting ready to go wake her."

"Do you mind if I do?"

"She would love it," I say. "I'll wait to pour your coffee until you get back.

"Thank you, Lila," she says.

I pour my own coffee once she leaves the room. I'm carrying the cup with me to the kitchen table when I feel the onset of dizziness hit. I stumble and drop the coffee to the floor, splashing the hot liquid down the front of my pajamas. I grab for something to hold onto, but there's nothing immediately nearby. I fall forward into the table, hitting the side of my head on the corner.

It seems like it takes forever for me to reach the floor. I have this feeling of being sucked into a vortex of some kind, my vision suddenly narrowing as a white haze slides over me. I hear myself gasp, and then any awareness of pain fades with the blackness overcoming me, until all I see is a small blip of white.

The trap door was there all along.

♪

Thomas

Not for Weaklings

"YOU'RE MOPING. You know that?"

I'm looking at my phone when Holden makes the assertion. I start to act as if I don't know what he's talking about, but what would be the point? "I just haven't been able to get in touch with her this morning."

"Isn't your mom there?"

"Yeah. She's not answering her cell either. It's weird."

"There are about a million explanations as to why. Would you please not latch onto the one that has them both stranded in a ditch somewhere?"

I roll my eyes and say, "I'm not that dramatic."

"You didn't use to be. That's for sure."

"Like you have any room at all to talk."

Holden smiles a little and shakes his head. "You're right."

The two of us are having breakfast in the restaurant on the first floor of our hotel. CeCe had wanted to get a run in before our bus leaves at nine for Charlotte, North Carolina.

"She'll call you any minute," Holden says, his tone now more sympathetic.

"The show went well last night," he says, in an obvious attempt to take my mind off Lila.

"Yeah," I say. "I know the venues we booked are smaller than the ones we played when we were with the label, but the crowds feel the same. It doesn't seem like people are any less interested in our music."

"That's what it feels like to me too," Holden says. "I have to admit it was a little scary taking that leap into independence, but it was the right thing to do, wasn't it?"

"I don't think they were leaving us a lot of choice, considering the new stuff they'd added to the contract and their refusal to see what's happening with streaming music."

"Think those two new songs played well last night?"

"Yeah. Really well."

"CeCe is excited about singing Lila's song tonight."

"I haven't told her yet," I say. "I thought I'd send her the video after the show."

"It's a good song," Holden says.

"Coming from you, I'm sure that would mean a lot to her. She really admires your writing."

Holden is quiet for a few moments, taking a sip from his coffee cup and then setting it back down. "I don't know if I've said exactly this, Thomas, but I'm glad you two found each other. She's been really good for you, hasn't she?"

"Yeah," I say, "she has. God knows I wasn't looking for it, because I had no idea that what we have could even exist, or at least for me. I guess seeing you and CeCe together should have clued me in that the real thing does happen. The longer I'm with her and Lexie, the more I worry that maybe something this real and amazing can't last forever."

"That's what love does, you know," Holden says. "It makes you scared. When you don't have it in your life, it's easy to be arrogant and dismissing of the whole thing. To think that if you had someone you cared about and they left you, eventually you would find someone else. But when you've found your soul mate, your other half, it doesn't feel like that. I can't even imagine myself living this life without CeCe. The truth is I wouldn't want to live it without her."

"Yeah, I get it." I move my food around on the plate, and then say, "I couldn't sleep last night after we got back from the show, so I was flipping through channels. There was this documentary on *Dateline* about a ship that sank off the coast of Africa several years ago. All the passengers had to be rescued. There was this older couple on board. He had just retired and this was the first of a bunch of trips, adventures they'd saved up for over the years. It took rescue helicopters four hours to reach the ship after it started sinking at sea. When it was their turn to get lifted in one of those harnesses that take two people at a time, the helicopter started reeling them up and the wife suddenly realized that her husband was slipping and he actually wasn't buckled in at all. She started trying to hold onto him, but he was too heavy, and there was no way she could keep him with her all the way up. So he finally told her that she had to let him go. Two hundred feet above the ocean, and they both realized she had no choice."

"Did she?" Holden asks, his gaze locked on mine.

"Yeah. He fell back into the ocean while she watched from up there. Can you imagine having to make a choice like that?"

"No," Holden says, shaking his head, "I really can't."

"The amazing thing was that he ended up living, but she had to be strong enough to let him go. If she hadn't, they might have both ended up dying with the harness breaking. Who knows?"

"At least their story had a happy ending," Holden says.

"I guess maybe the moral is that loving someone isn't for weaklings, is it?"

"No," Holden agrees. "It's definitely not."

♪

WE'VE BEEN ON THE bus almost two hours when I get a text back from Lila.

Sorry I missed your calls earlier and am just now checking in. It's been kind of a crazy day so far. All right if I give you a call later?

Sure, baby. Everything okay there?

Everything is fine. We've been having a wonderful visit with your mom. She's quite a cook.

She make you some of her famous biscuits?

Yes, she did. Oh my goodness.

Give Lexie and Mom a hug from me. Okay?

Okay.

Meanwhile, I'm going to sit here on my lonely bus and think about you. I miss you so much, baby.

I miss you.

We're on I-77 now, and there's not much to see of North Carolina outside the window. I pull a book out of my backpack and try to inject myself into the story, but I can't stop my mind from wandering to Lila and this weird feeling I have about not having talked with her this morning. Maybe I'm getting too overprotective.

I lean my head back against the seat and sigh, realizing I'm becoming unrecognizable even to myself.

I think about how different the touring used to feel and how I actually looked forward to it. But I'm not the same guy I was then. It doesn't feel okay with me being here and Lila and Lexie somewhere else.

And then suddenly I realize that I don't want to do this the way I did it before. If it's going to stay a part of my life, I want my girls with me. I'm not worried about what CeCe and Holden will think. Because there's no doubt that if anyone would understand what I'm feeling, it's the two of them.

♪

Lila

Until It Knocks

I HATE HOSPITALS.

I know it's not the right attitude to have, but the time I spent with Lexie in the hospital after she was born, seeing her hooked up to machines and tubes and being stuck with needles, I'd come to despise every moment of our time there. The constant smell of disinfectant, the strength of which could never quite conceal the scent of sickness. The hushed voices of doctors and nurses discussing the fate of a dying patient.

I'm in a room on the seventh floor. I see the sky outside the narrow window, a sliver of bright blue, a notable contrast to the sterile white walls surrounding my bed. There's an IV in my arm. I'm hooked up to some kind of machine that's monitoring my heart rate.

Mrs. Franklin is at the house with Lexie. I had pleaded with her to take Lexie home once the doctor in the ER told me I would need to be admitted for further testing. She had followed the ambulance to the hospital, bringing Lexie with her in my car. I know she hadn't had a choice because of the way everything happened, but when I finally opened my eyes to see Lexie's scared little face; I thought my heart would break in half from the pain of it.

We had agreed that it would be best to take Lexie back home, but Mrs. Franklin had been reluctant to go along with my plea not to tell Thomas anything until I knew something further.

The biggest show of the tour is scheduled for tonight in Charlotte, and I see no reason to jeopardize that when there really isn't anything Thomas can do here now.

A nurse walks into the room, carrying a tray of food with her. "How are you feeling, sweetie?"

"Better," I say. "Thank you."

"I thought you might like a little something to eat, since it's after lunch."

"I'm not very hungry," I say.

"How about if I set it up here in front of you, and you can change your mind in a bit or not?"

"Okay."

She checks my IV, and then looks at the machine and writes something on a clipboard hanging on the wall nearby.

"Do you know if my tests have been scheduled yet?" I ask.

"No, but how about I let you know as soon as we get word?"

"That would be great. Thank you so much."

She leaves the room then, her white nurse's shoes making no sound as she goes.

I feel the tears start to slide down my cheeks and brush them away with the back of my hand. I'm scared, and so very tempted to call Thomas, to change my mind and beg him to come back. I force myself not to, instead sending Macy a text and asking her if she's coming to town anytime soon.

In a few seconds, my phone dings.

I actually drove in this morning to spend a few days with Taylor. You're not going to believe it, but I was just getting ready to call you.

I hesitate for a moment, wondering if I should leave Macy out of this. Not give her reason to worry before I know anything. But I realize that I really need her right now. And so I tell her where I am and ask her to come.

♪

IT SEEMS AS if I barely blink before Macy walks through the door of the room. She's got that determined look on her face and a purpose in her walk that I recognize so well.

She walks straight over to the bed, sits down on the edge, and leans over to wrap me up in a hug. "What happened?" she asks, her voice unsteady.

"I passed out this morning in the kitchen. I've been having a little shortness of breath off and on lately."

"For how long?" she asks, leaning back to look down at me with worried eyes.

"The shortness of breath is new, but I've had a few episodes of dizziness here and there."

"Have you seen anyone about it?"

"I had a check up after we got back from our honeymoon. We decided to start trying for a baby, and I thought it would be a good idea."

"And nothing came up?" Macy asks.

"No, everything checked out fine."

"Could you be pregnant?" she asks.

"I don't know. They did a test when I was in the ER, but I haven't heard the results yet."

Macy looks relieved. "Well, maybe that's what this is all about. It would certainly make sense."

"Yeah," I say. "It could be."

"Is Thomas on the way back?"

"No. I don't want to tell him anything yet. They're in Charlotte tonight, and there's nothing for him to do here."

"He could just be with you."

"I'd like to call him right now, but there's a lot hanging on this show, and—"

"You know this isn't what he would want."

"As soon as I know something, I'll call him."

Macy looks doubtful, but knows me well enough to realize I'm not relenting on this right now.

"How long before they're supposed to let you know something?" she asks.

"No one seems to know."

"Give me the name of the doctor I should go heckle."

I smile. "I've missed you."

"I've missed you," Macy says, taking my hand.

"How's Taylor?"

Macy's expression softens, and her eyes get this dreamy look they take on anytime Taylor's name is mentioned. "He's still wonderful."

"So when are you moving to Nashville?"

"Believe it or not, I'm listening to Mama on this one."

"Wow," I say. "What is your mama saying?"

"Wait for the ring. Why is he going to buy the cow, if he can get the milk for free?"

I laugh for the first time today. "I love your mama."

"I love her too. She's always right. And I so don't want to mess this up."

"Anybody can see that he's crazy about you."

"That doesn't mean he'll want to marry me," Macy says, looking out the window.

I reach out and cover her hand with mine. "If he's as smart as I think he is, he will."

"Well, you might be just a slight bit prejudiced."

"I agree, but he'd be a lucky guy to have you."

The nurse who brought my lunch tray in earlier steps in to the room and says, "I just wanted to let you know the pregnancy test result came back, and it was negative. That's all we have so far. I'll be back in a bit, okay?"

I nod once, trying to force a smile to my lips, but it won't come. Instead, tears rush up and out of me and all of a sudden, I'm crying full out.

"Oh, honey," Macy says, pulling me up and into her arms. "It's okay. Everything's going to be okay. You and Thomas have plenty of time to make another baby."

I turn my face into her shoulder, but all of a sudden, I feel really scared. I wonder if Macy is right. I think I've been holding out hope that I was pregnant and that would explain what is happening. But now that it's been ruled out, a whole army of worries assault me.

"You remember that preacher who came for revival the summer we both turned thirteen?" Macy asks. "All of a sudden we were trying to figure out how we were supposed to act around boys and what we would do if they asked us out? All that ridiculous stuff we thought was such a big deal at the time?"

I nod a little, without raising my head.

"Remember what he said? Don't invite worry into your living room when the problem hasn't even knocked at your door yet. We don't even know if there really is a problem. Until we do, let's just not go there, okay?"

"Okay," I say, sitting up and wiping my eyes.

"Meanwhile," she says, "I'm right here. And I'm not going anywhere."

♪

Thomas

Beyond Value

THE SHOW IS sold out.

The venue holds 2000 people. Every seat is filled, and people are standing on the sides of the room and at the back. We're playing a lot of new music tonight, and the response is more than we had hoped for.

Holden gets complete credit for the success of this tour. He planned it down to the last detail, using our past success or failure in certain locations to decide whether we would play there again or not.

When CeCe introduces Lila's song *Boundaries*, she tells them the story about our honeymoon and the stewardess who seemed determined to ignore the ring on my finger. The women in the audience go wild when CeCe hits the chorus, and clearly the song has hit a chord with its intended audience.

As soon as we get back to the hotel, I send Lila the video that one of the guys in the crew had taken for me. I call her too but don't get an answer, so I send her a text.

Crowd loved your song tonight. Just sent you the video. What do you think?

When she hasn't replied by the time I get out of the shower, I try to call her again, but still don't get an answer. I send her another text.

Are you okay?

I'm starting to panic a little by the time the text dings through on my phone. It's late, but Lila always waits for us to talk before going to bed.

Hey. Yes. All good here. Sorry. I fell asleep.

Hey, babe. I was getting worried.

Just tired. How was the show?

Awesome. Your song went over big.

That's really cool.

59

Did you see the video?

Not yet.

CeCe tore it up.

She's amazing.

You're amazing. You wrote it. Want to talk?

Do you mind if we don't tonight? I'm kind of out of it.

Hard day?

A bit.

Are you all right?

Yes. Fine.

Lexie?

She's good. We miss you.

You couldn't miss me as much as I miss you.

I do.

Not possible.

I love you.

I love you, baby. Sweet dreams. Talk tomorrow?

Yes. Goodnight.

Goodnight.

♪

I TRY TO sleep, but at two a.m., I'm still awake, my mind refusing to shut off its worry.

Something hadn't felt right about Lila tonight. Beyond the fact that she always waits to hear from me before going to bed. I don't have anything real to base it on except a feeling.

I flip onto my side and try to blank my mind. It works for a few seconds, and then I'm imagining another scenario, Lila getting tired of me, tired of being at home alone, interested in someone else.

As soon as that thought raises its head, I vault off the bed and turn on the lamp.

I hate this new side of me. The one who doubts, worries, feels jealous. Is that what love does?

The answer comes to me on a bolt of honesty. That's what insecure love does.

Lila has never given me reason to feel insecure. So why do I?

And then the answer comes to me.

Because I've found something that is beyond value. There's no amount of money that can buy what I have. And I know as surely as I have ever known anything in my life that it is irreplaceable. A person is lucky to find what I've found in Lila once in his lifetime. Finding it twice? No.

Right behind that realization comes another.

I would never look for it again. Lila is once. She's only. She's given herself to me.

Why would I question it? It feels wrong to let anything like jealousy or possessiveness leech any of the color from the way we love each other.

A wave of peace washes over me, and I make a pact with myself not to question her love for me.

♪

Lila

Gratitude

I'M NOT GOING to feel sorry for myself.

I refuse to feel sorry for myself.

But here in this semi-dark hospital room, the quiet punctuated by the consistent beep of the machine monitoring my heart rate, I can't stop the tears welling in my eyes and sliding down my face. I reread the texts from Thomas, wishing I could call him, hear his voice. More than that, wishing he was here next to me. That I could lose myself in the strong comfort of the way he holds me, the way he makes me feel safe in a way I've never felt before.

I feel so guilty for deceiving him, for not telling him where I am. Even though I'm doing it for him. Or at least that's what I'm telling myself.

I wonder if it's true. Am I trying to prevent him from unnecessary worry, or am I scared that opening the door and letting him in will make all of this real in the most terrifying way possible? Is it right for me to keep this from him until I have answers?

I've gone back and forth in the past few hours. The selfish part of me is crying out for comfort, yearning for relief from the fear that grips at my insides, like a hawk clinging to the side of a cliff.

I don't want to be alone. And yet I'm not letting Thomas in.

Macy finally left at ten o'clock after I told her I didn't want her to stay, that I thought I would sleep better with no one in the room. I don't know that she believed me, but I was insistent enough that she finally gave in.

And I have to admit I'm now regretting it.

I hate the fear. Wish I could loosen its stranglehold. But my mind races with the possible scenarios ahead, and beyond any worry over pain or sickness is a terror of being without Lexie, without Thomas.

This is the note my brain is stuck on, and my tears are for that potential loss, not my own well-being.

Why is this happening? What did I do to deserve it?

I know the futility of the questions as soon as they present themselves. It's pointless to ask questions like these. Life doesn't come with any fairness guarantees. And I can think of any number of people I've met recently who are enduring hardships they never imagined enduring. I don't expect to be an exception.

But is it so wrong to want time with the two people I love more than I could ever love myself?

It's not wrong. I know that.

It might not be the future I had expected though. I might not be here to see Lexie grow up, to experience the seasons of change in my marriage to Thomas.

I wonder if this is why we found each other again. So that Lexie would have him if something happened to me. The thought releases a new torrent of tears from deep inside me. But this time, they aren't tears of fear or worry or hopelessness. They are tears of gratitude.

♪

Lila

Far Away on a Beach

AN ORDERLY PUSHES a gurney into my room at 6:30 the next morning.

I finally fell asleep at some point during the night. The last time I looked at the clock, it was 3:15, and I am groggy and exhausted when he and a nurse help me from the bed.

"They got you in bright and early this morning," the nurse says on a cheerful note. "This way, you'll beat the traffic."

I nod, unable to force words past my lips. I lie down, and they tuck the white sheets in around me. With my arms at my sides, I feel mummified. Anxiety shortens my breath, and I decide that the only way I can get through this without having a panic attack is to close my eyes and only open them if I absolutely have to.

This is something I learned to do after my mom died. After my dad killed my mom, I correct myself. The image of her lying on our living room floor, blood pooled around her as if her entire body's worth had somehow managed to escape her veins, is a picture I have never been able to erase from my mind. I realized then that there are some things in this world a person should never see. Things that will be so seared into a memory that there is no escaping their forever effects.

I see her face, her beautiful, too pale face, and the way she had looked that day. I have never been able to replace it with a memory of her when she was alive, vibrant and loving. I've wanted to. Have tried to. But it's never worked.

I decided somewhere along the way that I wouldn't look at things I can't emotionally handle. I don't look at car accidents when traffic is detoured around them. I don't look at the commercials of dogs and cats at the pound because their faces haunt me. When there's something difficult that I have to get through, I close my eyes until it's over.

That's what got me through the months after my mother's death. The nights I spent in a psychiatric hospital, fighting back panic attacks and nightmares.

That's what I do now. Behind my closed lids, I picture the beach on Anguilla. Thomas's sun-browned body stretched out next to mine on the white sand. Pelicans flying lazily above us, dipping into the ocean now and then to scoop out a fish. I feel the warm sun on my shoulders and hear the gentle lull of the waves licking at the shore.

My anxiety lifts and leaves me. I'm not here in this hospital, fearing the unknown. I'm far away, with Thomas, the man I love.

I will get through this.

I will.

♪

Lila

Gamechanger

MACY IS SITTING with me in my hospital room that afternoon, trying to distract me with movie-star gossip from *People* magazine when a doctor walks in.

He's small and balding, his face a mask of seriousness. He has a very *Duck-Dynasty* type beard, and I wonder with a near giggle of hysteria if it is an unconscious attempt to make up for what has disappeared from his hairline. His voice when he speaks is nearly impatient, as if in coming here, he is missing out on something he would far rather be doing.

"Mrs. Franklin?"

"Yes?" I say.

"I'm Dr. Zimmerman. The cardiologist referred to your case."

"It's nice to meet you," I say, unable to think of anything else to say, even though I'm pretty sure neither of us is really happy to meet the other.

"We have your test results back. Is it okay to discuss them now?" he asks, glancing at Macy.

I nod in agreement.

"I wish I had better news for you," he says.

Macy stands from her chair, as if she has been ejected from it. "What do you mean?" she asks.

I reach for her hand and squeeze hard, saying, "Go ahead, Dr. Zimmerman."

"You have myocarditis. A rather advanced case of it, I'm afraid."

"Myo—what is that?" Macy asks, her question underscored with outrage. I can feel its surge in our joined hands.

He looks at me when he answers. "It's an inflammation of the middle layer of the heart wall, the myocardium."

"What causes it?" I ask, barely knowing where to begin.

"Usually a viral infection," he says. "Sometimes it's bacterial. In your case, we believe it's bacterial and will be treating you with antibiotics. We'll start with IV infusions, and you will need to spend a couple of days in the hospital."

I think about Lexie and immediately ask, "Is that necessary? Can I take the medicine at home?"

"Mrs. Franklin, I don't want to alarm you, but this is apparently something you've had for a while. It is in your best interest to be aggressive with treatment, and it's better if we can monitor you here in the hospital."

Macy squeezes my hand. "Then that's what you'll do. Don't worry about Lexie. I'll be here for you in whatever way you need."

Dr. Zimmerman gives Macy a look of approval. "Let's get your treatment underway and see how you are in a couple of days. Okay?"

"Yes," I say, realizing it is the only choice I have.

♪

MACY IS NOT a woman who cries. She never has been. Not even when my mom died. Or at her funeral.

She's just strong like that. Able to be the shoulder to cry on. She has been for as long as I've known her.

But as soon as Dr. Zimmerman leaves the room, pulling the door shut behind him, Macy looks at me with an expression of disbelief, and she starts to cry.

"This can't be happening, Lila. It's not right."

"Macy—"

"You just got married. You and Thomas—"

"It's okay," I interrupt her. "He didn't say I was dying."

"But it sounds serious. Lila, you have to call Thomas. You can't keep this from him."

I don't say anything for a few long moments. I want to call him. Now. Tell him how much I need him. How scared I am. But I'm not going to let myself do it. "He'll be home in two weeks, Macy. There's no need to mess up the tour. If you can help with Lexie, everything will be fine. And hopefully, by the time he gets here, I'll be well on the road to recovery."

She wants to argue with me. I see it on her face. But Macy is nothing if not the truest kind of friend. And she knows this is what I want. So it's what she does.

♪

IT'S NOT SO BAD, the few days I'm in the hospital. Maybe it's because the IVs of antibiotics are a symbol of what I need to do to get better. I do exactly what the nurses ask of me, and they name me one of their best patients ever.

An older nurse with white hair and thick rubber-soled shoes that squeak on the hospital floor tells me this one afternoon when she is changing my IV. "You'd be amazed by how many people come in here sick but completely unwilling to do what the doctors tell them to do. Sometimes, I wonder why they waste their time or our time."

"Habits are hard to change," I say.

"That is true. But the game changer on that is being told that unless you change your behavior, you're going to die. More often than not, that doesn't even get them."

"I want to get better," I say.

"I can see that, honey," she says, empathy underlining the words. "You have children?"

"A daughter. And a husband."

"Ah. How old is your daughter?"

"She just turned ten."

"Wonderful age, isn't it?" she says, testing the drip on the IV.

"Every year has been a wonderful age with her."

"Aren't you the lucky one? I haven't seen your husband yet."

"He's out of town for work."

She leans back and gives me a look. "Does he know you're here?"

I shake my head, not meeting her eyes.

"What kind of work does he do?"

"He's in a band."

"Would I have heard of him?"

"Maybe."

"Shoot."

"Barefoot Outlook. Thomas is my husband."

She stops what she's doing and raises her eyebrows at me. "Girl, you lucky thing."

I smile. "I am that."

"By not telling him what's going on with you, are you protecting him or yourself?"

I consider the question, answering honestly. "Both of us, I guess. We haven't been married too long."

"Can I be straight with you, sweetie?"

I nod without meeting her gaze.

"I've been a nurse for a lot of years. I've seen just about every kind of life-altering situation you can imagine. There's one thing I know. People need their support systems. We humans are fragile. If we think we have a fight ahead of us, it's easy to start thinking it's going to require more than we have to get through it."

"I'm okay," I say. "This tour is important to his career and to the group."

"Is this the decision he would want you to make?"

I don't even have to think about the answer. There's no question in my mind what he would want. What he would do. Knowing that is enough for me.

♪

Thomas

Home

MY FLIGHT GETS into Nashville on Sunday afternoon.

It's been almost a month since I left, but it feels like a year. I can hardly wait to see my girls. Excitement buzzes in my veins with the inebriating effect of whiskey, and I feel as if I am going to come out of my skin if I don't set my eyes on them now.

I walk through the tube connecting the plane to the terminal, and there they are, Lila standing, Lexie in her wheelchair. They both smile instantly, and I can't get to them fast enough. I lean in and kiss Lila on the mouth, putting one arm around her and dropping onto my knee to hug and kiss Lexie.

Lexie's smile lights me up, and the tears in Lila's eyes tie my heart in a knot.

"I don't ever want to be away from you again," I say, kissing Lila once more.

"I don't want to be away from you either," she says, slipping her arms around my neck and hugging me hard.

"Let's go home," I say, and for the first time in my adult life, that word has real meaning to me.

♪

"I HAD NO idea you could cook like this," I say, walking up behind Lila to slip my arm around her waist and kiss her neck. Brownie follows me across the kitchen, dropping onto the floor beside us. He's followed me room to room since we walked in the door.

"A girl needs to have a few secrets," she says. "Actually, the truth is, your mom gave me some lessons. She should have her own cooking show."

"I'd have to agree with you there."

"I asked her what your three favorite things were that she cooked for you. And that's what we're having tonight."

"Macaroni and cheese."

"Check."

"Cornbread with honey."

"Check."

"Apple pie with vanilla ice cream."

"Check."

I laugh and turn her around to face me, dipping in to kiss her as I have wanted to kiss her since the moment I saw her in the airport. The kiss is long and deep and full of my need for her. I make no pretense of hiding it, whispering in her ear, "As much as I am looking forward to eating this incredible meal you've fixed, I really don't know how much longer I can wait to get you alone."

She turns her face to mine and kisses me softly. I feel something different in her, but I can't place what it is. I tip her chin up, force her to meet my eyes. "Is something wrong, baby?"

"Everything is right," she says. "You're home."

♪

BUT SHE'S QUIET throughout dinner.

I tell stories about some of the things that happened on the tour. Lexie holds my hand throughout the entire meal, as if she's determined not to let me out of her sight. Which makes me happy.

Lila tells me what Lexie has been doing in school and how pleased her teachers are with her progress. Lexie beams beneath the praise, and I love them both so much that it actually hurts.

It's almost ten by the time we get the kitchen cleaned up and Lexie in bed. I read her a story and don't leave the room until she is fast asleep. Even then, I linger at the side of her bed, watching the rise and fall of her breathing, feeling so very thankful to know this beautiful child is ours.

Lila appears in the doorway, and I look around to meet her understanding gaze. "She's amazing," I say.

"She is," Lila agrees.

I take her hand as we leave the room, pulling the door closed behind us. In the living room, I turn her to face me, running my hands through her long hair and breathing in the scent of her. "I didn't think it was possible to miss someone as much as I missed you."

"I missed you more," she says.

Her smile is tentative, and I am again hit with the feeling that something is wrong. "When are you going to tell me?"

She looks up at me with wide eyes. "What do you mean?"

"Lila. I can feel it. Something is different."

She walks over to the sofa and sits down. "We do need to talk, Thomas."

I move around the coffee table to take the spot next to her. My mind has raced ahead to a dozen different possibilities. Lila has met someone else. She wants a divorce. She doesn't want to be in Nashville anymore.

"I'm sick," she says.

And the bottom falls right out of my world.

♪

Lila

Do-Overs

HONESTLY, THE LOOK on his face is like a knife in my heart.

I want to spare him this, cover up all the possible scenarios with assurances that it's nothing serious, that everything will be all right.

But now that I've gotten myself to this place of admission, I can't keep any of it from him a moment longer. I need to share the burden, ask him to carry some of it for me.

For the past week or so, I've felt myself begin to stumble under its weight; the worry and fear of what might lie ahead creeping up from its dark place to snag me with its sharp talons.

"What's wrong?" he asks, his voice not sounding like his voice at all.

I meet his gaze directly. "I have myocarditis."

He shakes his head a little, as if he doesn't know where to begin.

"A couple of weeks ago, when your mom was here, I woke up with some dizziness and shortness of breath. I passed out in the kitchen and your mom called 911. I was in the hospital for a few days—"

"What?" he asks, as if I'm speaking a language he doesn't understand.

"I wanted to tell you, Thomas, but I knew how important this first tour was for all of you."

"You were hospitalized, and you didn't tell me? My mom didn't tell me?"

"I asked her not to."

"Lila," he says. "How could you do that?"

"I thought it could wait. Until you got back."

He stands up fast and bumps the coffee table with his shin. "Shit," he says and moves across the room, turning to look back at me with disbelief on his face.

"Thomas—"

"We're married," he interrupts. "We're not supposed to have secrets."

"I didn't want it to be a secret. I just wanted—"

"—to take care of it on your own? Without me? The way you did the first nine years of our daughter's life?"

"No. That's not it."

"What else could it be?" he asks, backing away with a raised hand. "We both said for better or worse. I meant it, Lila. But you're still shutting me out."

"I don't mean to. I was trying to do the best thing for—"

"Closing me out isn't the best thing for any of us, Lila!"

He's angry now, and I flinch a little beneath the punch of the words. "I wasn't closing you out, Thomas."

"I don't know what else you would call it, Lila."

He walks out of the room then, and I hear the sound of the keys as he grabs them from the bowl in the foyer. I get up and go after him, but he's already slamming the door and striding down the walkway to the truck.

I stand with my hand on the knob, looking through the glass and watching him go. I wonder now what I was thinking, how I could expect him to be anything other than upset with me.

I want to rewind the clock and do it over again. But I can't. That's the thing about choices. We don't get do-overs. I should know that by now.

♪

Thomas

No Way to Leave a Lady

I DRIVE OUT of the city, speeding, and for once, not caring if I get caught.

I don't think about where I'm going and somehow end up in Leiper's Fork outside of the city, pulling the truck into the parking lot at Puckett's Grocery and Restaurant. I get out and go inside. I find a table at the back corner, ordering myself a coffee when the waitress comes. She smiles at me, recognition in her eyes, but she doesn't call me on it, and I more than appreciate it.

I take a sip of the hot liquid, too fast, and burn my tongue in the process. I set the cup down and lean back in the chair, folding my arms across my chest and replaying the conversation with Lila at the house.

My heart immediately increases its pace, and I try to hold onto my anger because I'm too scared to look beyond it.

But here, alone, with my thoughts, the anger can't seem to get a foothold.

I text Holden and ask him to meet me out here. I know he and CeCe just got back into town. They were on a later flight than mine, and I'm a little surprised when he says it'll take him thirty minutes, but he's coming.

I've just finished my second cup of coffee when he walks in the door. The same waitress who cut me a break cuts him one too, smiling a nice smile at Holden, but waving him back to my table.

Holden crosses the room with long strides, a look of concern on his face when he slides onto the chair at the table. "Hey, man. Why aren't you home, making love to your wife?"

"That's definitely where I thought I'd be tonight," I say.

"What happened?" Holden asks, concern now underlining his words.

I don't even know where to start, so I begin in the middle. "I'm such an ass."

"I'll reserve judgment until I hear the facts."

"Lila was sick while we were gone. In the hospital, actually."

He sits back a little, confused. "And she didn't tell you?"

I shake my head.

"Well, it doesn't take a genius to figure out why," he says without hesitating. "You know she didn't want to mess up the tour."

"But how could she keep it from me?"

"Because she loves you and was trying to do what she thought was best for you."

"What's best for her is what's best for me."

"Is she all right, man? What was wrong?"

"She said myocarditis."

"She's been treated?"

"Yeah. I think so."

"Is she better?"

"I don't know. We didn't exactly finish talking."

"That ain't no way to leave a lady," Holden says, shaking his head.

"I know. Shit. I've made a mess of this."

"Hey, man. I get it. You want her to need you. To turn to you. Like she didn't do when she found out she was pregnant. I don't blame you. But I'm betting this really wasn't about that. I'm betting she really was doing it for you. That's what love does, you know. Makes you want to put the other one first. She loves you, Thomas. Any fool can see that."

"Any fool except this fool."

"Go home and make this right. If she's not well yet, get busy helping her do just that."

"One of these days, you're going to start charging me."

"I might just do it."

I look away for a moment, and then say what I don't want to say. "What if she's not all right?"

"Don't go there."

I push back my chair and stand, as anxious now to get home as I was earlier to get away. I drop a twenty on the table, and Holden and I walk outside together.

"Thanks for coming," I say. "Somehow you always help me get my thoughts straight."

"Will you let me know something in the morning?"

"I will. Later."

"Later."

♪

Lila

If Wishes Made It So

I LIE IN our bed, staring out the window where the starlit sky is visible through the curtains.

It's after midnight when I hear the front door open and shut. I breathe a sigh of relief and close my eyes with the hope that he'll come to bed and not sleep on the couch.

I hear his footsteps in the hall and then the click of our bedroom door. He walks into the room, and even in the dark, I sense him standing at the side of the bed, silent.

"I'm sorry," I say.

He sits down next to me, reaches for my hand and laces his fingers through mine. "Tell me," he says. "Tell me everything."

♪

I DO. And somewhere during my explanation, Thomas slides into bed beside me, pulling me in against him and wrapping his arms tight around my waist. I am anchored to him, both physically and emotionally, and I don't know how I ever imagined I could get through this without him.

I tell him everything the doctors have told me, how the antibiotics have helped, but there is some damage to my heart.

"What does that mean?" he asks, his voice husky with emotion.

"They don't fully know at this point," I say. "But there's a possibility I might need a transplant someday."

"Lila," he says softly, my name breaking in the middle. He turns me to face him then, and I think if he could absorb me into himself, he would. His grief is a tangible thing between us, his fear so anguished that I feel it cut through me.

"I'm sorry," I say again, because I don't know what else to say.

"You have nothing to be sorry for," he says softly against my ear.

"This isn't how I expected our life to go."

"It's going to be okay, baby."

"How do you know?"

"Because it has to be. It just has to be."

♪

Thomas

The Way It's Supposed to Be

I MAKE SOME calls Monday morning until I find a producer whose daughter is a patient of the top cardiologist in town. He gets us in to see the doctor at two o'clock that afternoon.

I tell Lila about the appointment after I get back from taking Lexie to school. I find her in the office, checking emails. She looks up at me and smiles, but it's not her normal smile. I would give anything to be able to turn the clock back to those days after we were first married, when I could not imagine that we would be facing something like this. When life had felt like an open book before us, the pages waiting to be filled with the happy chapters of our lives.

We don't talk all the way to the cardiologist's office, the silence heavy with our own undeniable worry.

Once we've checked in, a nurse with kind eyes leads us to Dr. Maston's office. She knocks once at the door before we hear a deep voice answer, "Please, come in."

"Thank you, Selena," he says, standing up to offer Lila and me seats in front of his desk.

The nurse nods once, then steps out of the room, closing the door behind her.

"It's very nice to meet you both," Dr. Maston says. "Although I obviously wish it weren't under these circumstances."

"Thank you for seeing us so quickly," I say. "We appreciate it so much."

"You're very welcome. I've had a preliminary look at your case, Mrs. Franklin. How have you been feeling?

"Lila, please," she says. "Pretty well."

"The antibiotics have helped?"

"Yes."

"But?"

She hesitates, and I feel her reluctance to go on, but then she says, "I just don't have my normal energy level."

"Umm," he says, looking down at the file in front of him. "I understand Dr. Zimmerman has told you of the notable damage to your heart."

"Yes," she says softly.

I flinch at the exchange—notable damage—wondering if I have somehow downplayed the significance of this.

"This is the issue we must deal with," the doctor says matter-of-factly.

"Yes," I say, hearing the urgent note in my own voice. "Tell us what we need to do."

He looks at me then with eyes full of understanding, eyes that have no doubt seen countless other people sitting across the desk from him with the same note of desperation in their voices that I know he now hears in mine.

"As I'm sure you both know, there is no simple answer."

I reach across and take Lila's hand, as much to right myself as to comfort her.

"We can handle difficult," I say. "We just need to know where to begin."

"There are medicines we will try, of course. Depending on the individual, we have varying levels of success with them."

"As a permanent fix?" I ask, unable to disguise the hopeful plea in my question.

Dr. Maston shakes his head with a somber look. "As a doctor, I never want to assume that a patient's situation will be a case where the most extreme thing will go wrong. Because sometimes it doesn't happen. But, on the other hand, I feel an obligation to give my patients the opportunity to understand the fight they might be facing. For many, it is a fight."

I try to pull in a deep breath, but the air seems to be stuck in my chest. I feel Lila squeeze my hand, and I force myself to ask, "Will my wife need a transplant?"

He doesn't answer for several moments, looking down at the papers containing Lila's history. "Based on my experience, my guess at this point would be yes."

I let each of the words process, each like a nail in my resolve to do whatever we need to do to make Lila well again. To get her back to normal. "Please," I say. "Just tell us where to start."

♪

WE LEAVE THE office and drive in silence for the first fifteen minutes. I've asked CeCe to pick Lexie up at school and I take the Interstate out of the city and find us a country road to slow down on.

"Thomas," Lila says, "it's okay."

"No, baby, nothing is okay right now."

"Can we find a place to stop?"

"Sure," I say. It takes a mile or two, but I spot a wide green hayfield with its narrow dirt road turnoff.

I cut the engine, and Lila opens the truck door and slides out.

She walks across the field, dropping her head back to stare up at the blue sky as if she wants to drink in its expanse.

I get out and follow her. When I finally catch up, I scoop her into my arms and carry her until we reach the enormous old oak tree at the far corner of the pasture. I lean my back against the trunk and slide down with Lila still in my arms, cradling her to me. She presses her face to my neck, and I feel the tears on her cheek. I think if it is possible for a heart to break into a thousand pieces, mine is doing exactly that.

The sun has begun to drop in the Tennessee sky when Lila says, "It's going to be all right, Thomas. Whatever happens, it will be okay."

"Not if I'm here without you. That won't be okay."

"But Lexie will need you."

"Baby, don't," I say, my voice cracking.

"We have to talk about it," she says softly. "Maybe this is why we found each other again. Because Lexie will need you."

I'm crying fully now, tears streaming down my face, sobs breaking free from my throat.

Lila tightens her grip around my neck, and although I can tell she's trying not to, she's crying as hard as I am. We're no comfort to each other, but our pain is mutual.

"I'm so scared, Thomas," she says in little more than a whisper.

"I know," I say. "So am I. How can this be happening?"

I hear the anger in my voice, and I want to yell at the sky, scream at the breeze lifting the grass in the field.

"We have to think of Lexie first. I have to know that she will be with you. That you will always take care of her."

"Lila, please, you're killing me."

"Promise me, Thomas. I can't face any of this without knowing that."

"With my life, Lila. I will protect her with my life."

"That's all I need to know," she says. "Thank you."

She lifts her face to mine and kisses me, the salt of our tears mingling. I feel her gratitude, and I know that I am nothing if not a fraud. I also promised to protect Lila.

And we both know how that's turning out.

♪

WE SEE DR. MASTON two more times that week. He wants to conduct a couple more tests on Lila. On Friday, we go to his office to discuss the medications he recommended trying for her.

I hate how serious they sound, and how serious he is when he lays out the possible side effects.

It is just another blatant reminder of what we are facing, and every time I start to think I have a handle on my anger, these moments make me realize that I do not.

Lila squeezes my hand while we listen, and I feel a stab of shame for the fact that I should be the one comforting her, not the other way around.

When we leave the office, we walk outside and get in the truck. Lila clutches the bag of medicines to her lap, as if it is a lifeline to which she is clinging. I guess, in all reality, it is. I can barely stop myself from pitching the whole bag out the window like a child who hates the toy he's been given to play with.

"I despise the thought of you having to take all of those pills."

"I'm not crazy about it either," she says. "But what is the saying? It's better than the alternative?"

I lean across the seat and kiss her on the mouth. "It's not supposed to be like this."

"Our new normal," she says.

"If I could switch places with you—"

"I know you would," she interrupts me. "But I wouldn't want you to."

I can't speak. I can barely breathe.

"I need for you to know something, Thomas."

"What?" I ask, not recognizing my own voice.

"I would understand if you don't want to do this."

"This?"

"Stay with me. You didn't sign on for a wife with a failing heart."

"Don't say that. And where else in the world would I be than with you?"

"You have a full life, Thomas—"

"You are my life, Lila. You and Lexie are my life."

I feel her collapse a little, as if the words she's just said took all the resolve she could manage. "I'm sorry," she says. "I'm so sorry."

"You have nothing to be sorry about, baby. Nothing."

"I thought we would have so much time," she says, crying softly.

"Shh," I say, rubbing her hair with the palm of my hand. "We will. Temporary roadblock. That's all."

But I don't think either of us finds my words much comfort.

"I think we're going to need some help for the foreseeable future," she says. "Your mom and Macy know what's going on. Can we tell CeCe and Holden but not anyone else?"

"Sure we can."

She shakes her head as if she is trying to come to terms with a truth neither of us wants to face. "I never imagined myself being this fragile person."

"You're not fragile," I say. "You're the strongest person I know."

"Part of me still feels strong, but I'm beginning to realize exactly what all of this means. I think we're both going to have to get to that point, Thomas," she says then, looking directly at me.

I want to ask her exactly what it is she wants me to accept. That she's ill. That she might die. But I can't accept that. And I'm too afraid to ask whether she wants me to.

I reach across the seat and take her hand. "We'll get through this, Lila. We will."

She squeezes my hand and nods. But I can feel her uncertainty. And I can't deny that it's like we have been caught up in some kind of funnel, pulling us down, down, even as we stretch our arms to the sky in a silent plea for mercy.

♪

WE DRIVE OVER to CeCe and Holden's house to pick up Lexie. While she's in the living room watching a TV show, I tell them we'd like to talk about something for a minute, and we go into the kitchen, standing around the island in the center of the room.

In a neutral voice that doesn't even sound like my own, I tell them what has happened, what Lila is facing, and how we hope we'll be able to ask for their help with Lexie as needed.

No one says anything until I've finished talking.

Tears well in CeCe's eyes, and she walks around the island to put her arms around Lila and hug her tight. And then they're both crying, while Holden and I look on, unable to do a damn thing to change any of it.

♪

Lila

The List

FOR THE NEXT few months, I feel as if I am living someone else's life.

I walk around in my body each day, speak with my voice, confide in my husband, and cherish every minute of my time with my daughter.

And yet I feel almost like I'm outside myself, separate, already looking in at something I'm not going to be a part of forever. It's as if I'm emotionally receding from the world, becoming a ghost in my own life.

I find that I don't want to be anywhere except with Thomas and Lexie. My time with them feels precious in the way of something I know can't last forever, and is slipping through my fingers.

I don't know how to act. Do I continue my habit of writing every day? Does it matter whether I have anything to say? Is that a waste of time? Should I be making a list of things I would like to do with my husband and daughter before I die?

The first time I let the word run through my mind, I felt a wall break inside me. Behind it came a torrent of anger and grief so fierce that I locked myself in the bathroom and screamed until I was hoarse. When Thomas got home and asked me if I was getting a cold, I told him I thought it was allergies.

After that, I deliberately forced the word into my mind over and over again. Die. Die. Die. Until I began to be able to think it without the bottom falling out of my stomach. It's not as if we don't all know that this will be the eventual outcome for us. But I guess we have some sense of entitlement that we will live an average lifespan. Celebrate the anniversaries of our marriage. Seeing our children grow up. And when we realize that might not be the case, we feel cheated.

But have I been? I mean, really? I can make any number of

comparisons that would support an argument that I haven't been cheated.

I'm married to the man of my dreams. I have a child I would give my life for. And I have the certainty of knowing that she will be loved and taken care of after I'm gone.

And so this is what I latch onto whenever my thoughts start to detour into self-pity. Given the choice, I want to be here with the people I love. I don't want to leave them. But if that is what happens, I want to leave both my husband and my daughter with the memory of me without bitterness or anger. I want to be at peace with my life's end, whenever it comes.

So I start my list. And I order each of the things I would like to do, by what would be most meaningful to all three of us.

I'm working on it one night and fall asleep with the pen and journal on my lap. I come awake and find the lamp still on. Thomas is standing by the bed with my list in his hand. He's reading it with tears streaming down his face.

I reach out to take his hand in mine. "We'll do them together."

He turns off the lamp and slides in beside me, pulling me into his arms, my back to his chest. He buries his face against my neck, and I feel him crying, even though he makes no sound at all.

♪

Thomas

Story Told

I'M MAKING BREAKFAST for Lila one Saturday morning when my phone rings. I set the coffee pot on the tray and pull the phone from my pocket, spotting Holden's face on the screen and putting the call on speaker.

"Hey."

"Sorry to call so early," he says.

"I'm up. Everything okay?"

"Yeah. It's just something I thought you'd like to know about. There's a post on our Facebook page asking about the rumor that Lila is sick."

"What does it say?"

"I think it's a reporter fishing."

"Let's ignore it. Or delete it."

"I was going to, but other people have started asking, so short of deleting the whole page, I don't think it will help."

"Shit."

"How do you want to address it, Thomas?" Holden asks in a sympathetic voice.

I sit down at the kitchen table, as if all the air has been let out of me. "There's no running from it, is there?"

Holden sighs, and I hear his frustration, know how much he would change this for me if he could. "What can I do?"

"If I could think of something, I would ask it of you. Believe me."

"And I would do it."

"I know."

"Do you want to ignore the questions or come up with an answer?"

"Lila asked for privacy. She doesn't want this to be public."

"It sucks," Holden says. "You know they'll keep digging until they get something. It might be best to lead with the truth rather than letting them create it."

"I'll write something up after I talk to Lila and send it to you."

"Thomas?"

"Yeah?"

"Are you okay? I mean really okay."

I don't say anything for a few moments, and then, "How can someone with a heart so good need a new one?"

But Holden doesn't have an answer any more than I do. And in the wake of his silence, I wish I hadn't asked the question.

♪

OVER THE NEXT few days, the story grows. What started on our Facebook page, gets picked up by other sites until it metastasizes to the major media outlets, and our phone starts to ring nonstop.

"We don't have to talk to them," I say on the second morning of the incessant ringing. We're in the kitchen getting Lexie's lunch ready for school.

"They don't seem willing to be ignored," she says in a low voice, keeping her gaze on the peanut butter sandwich she's making. "And some of the speculation on my possible demise is becoming humorous."

"It's none of their business," I say, anger edging into my voice.

"No. But that doesn't mean they'll leave it alone. Take the call, Thomas. It's okay."

"Lila—"

"It would be nice for the phone to stop ringing."

I pick up the cordless from the island in the middle of the room and walk to my office before clicking it on. And our story gets told.

♪

Lila

Greater Plan

IT'S WEIRD TO READ about yourself as if you're reading about a stranger.

The day after Thomas talks to the first reporter, the main Nashville newspaper includes a piece titled "Wife of Barefoot Outlook Star Needs New Heart."

I let myself absorb the headline, waiting for anger or outrage to hit me. But they don't. And that's when I realize I've accepted what's happening to me. I don't want to accept it. I don't want it to be. But there it is in black and white. Undeniable.

My phone rings, and Macy's face flashes on the screen. "Hey," I say, trying to inject some cheer into my voice.

"Hey."

"You saw it?"

"Yeah. They so totally suck."

"It's their job."

"No one should have a job that involves sensationalizing someone else's pain."

"It doesn't change the truth of it."

"How are you?" Macy asks, her voice a little flat, as if she's siphoned out the emotion.

"I'm okay."

"Hey, it's me. Really."

"Someone else has to die for me to live." My voice breaks in half, and I can't say more.

"Oh, Lila," Macy says, tears infusing my name.

"I don't even know how to pray about living because I'll be asking for someone else to leave this world so I can stay."

"You can't think of it like that, honey."

"How else can I think about it?"

Macy sighs, as if what she is about to say is hard to get out. "I believe we each have our time. And Lila, if you stay, if any of us stay, then it isn't our time. Your needing a heart won't be the reason someone else leaves this world."

I consider her words. "Do you really believe that?"

"I do," she says. "The truth is none of us knows how long we have to be here. It literally could be until the next minute or until we're ninety-three. I don't believe this world is ready to lose you yet, Lila. So let's have faith that however this plays out is part of a greater plan."

"I want to believe that."

"Then do. Please. You deserve the peace of that, my sweet friend."

"What would I do without you?" I ask.

"I love you, Lila."

"I love you too."

♪

Thomas

Out of the Blue

THREE MONTHS HAVE come and gone since the day I learned my wife is sick.

It seems like three seconds and three lifetimes all at once. I don't know how to explain it except that time is on hold. And the waiting, the not knowing, that is the part that is becoming unbearable. I want to live each day with the intent of wringing as much from it as possible, but at the back of any joy we manage to find is the curtain of black, of uncertainty and dread.

Life has become about the unexpected, the next monster to jump out of the closet. And so, the message on the Barefoot Outlook Facebook page asking me to call a number at the Red Onion State Prison on a Friday afternoon at two o'clock probably shouldn't have been much of a surprise.

Lila had told me that this was the supermax prison where her father was serving time. I had actually looked it up once to see what it was like. It opened in 1998 and houses about 800 prisoners. Wikipedia claims the prison houses the worst of the worst. It's hard to imagine that Lila's father qualifies as one of those prisoners. But based on what he did, he does.

I consider telling her about the message, asking her if she wants me to call. But I know what her answer will be. And I decide that I will find out what he wants before telling her anything about it.

I make the call from my truck, waiting while the phone rings a number of times.

"Hello." A man finally answers, the word rusty as if he doesn't use his voice often.

"This is Thomas Franklin," I say.

"Thank you for calling me. I'm Michael Bellamy, Lila's—"

"—father. Yes, I know."

"I'll have to be brief since I only have a couple of minutes on this payphone."

"What can I do for you, Mr. Bellamy?"

"I know I have no right to ask this of you, but could you possibly come here to see me?"

I hesitate, no idea what to say. "Why?" I ask, too startled to edit my abruptness.

"Is it true about Lila?"

I hesitate, but then seeing no point in being dishonest, I say, "Yes."

He doesn't reply for several long moments, and I wonder if I should have cushioned my answer a little more.

"I need to talk with you," he says finally. "Can you please come? Next Tuesday at one o'clock?"

"Mr. Bellamy, I don't know what we could possibly have to talk about."

"It's important."

"I can't promise you," I say.

"Lila would never approve. Please don't tell her."

"You're putting me in a very difficult position."

"I understand that. I have to go now," he says. "I hope to see you next week."

And then he's gone. I sit long after the call ends, wondering what the right thing to do is. I can't imagine telling Lila that I've talked with her father, because I know how upset she would be, and I don't want to give her any more stress to handle. I tell myself I don't have to decide now. To go without telling Lila would make me feel like a traitor. Which makes it clear that I already have my answer.

♪

Thomas

Promises

WHICH IN NO WAY explains why I find myself making the five-and-a-half hour drive from Nashville to Wise County Virginia the following Tuesday morning.

I leave the city at six o'clock, planning to arrive by lunchtime. I asked Holden to cover for me, and I've created a small maze of lies with Lila in order to pull this off. The guilt is a knot in my throat I can barely swallow past.

I don't know that I can even explain to myself why I'm going. I've gone back and forth on the decision, wavering between telling Lila and not telling her. I know she would never have agreed to the visit, and I guess somewhere in the back of my mind, I need to hear what he wants. Does he know something that might help Lila? What if he does and I don't go?

I try to blank my mind of everything except getting this over with, cranking the music and just driving, focusing on the highway ahead. I arrive at the remote prison just before noon. I recall the Wikipedia fact that Pittston Coal Company had donated several hundred acres of land for the facility on Red Onion Mountain. Of the prisoners housed here, a huge percentage of them live in solitary confinement.

I've never actually been to a prison before, and at the sight of this one, I feel my heart kick up a notch. It is a grim place, intimidatingly stark and bleak, all concrete, steel, and wire. It's a cloudy day, and the grey of the sky seems to match the setting. I park the truck in the visitor's lot and wonder if I'm crazy to be here.

Before giving myself a chance to change my mind, I walk to the entrance, pulling a ball cap low on my head in the hope that I won't be recognized. This is not a visit I want to see in the papers.

Inside the building, I wait in line behind a mother here to visit her son. She's driven seven hours. She makes small-talk with me while the stern-faced man behind the front desk types something into the computer and then buzzes someone to bring the prisoner she is there to see to the visiting room. She starts to follow a uniformed officer, but turns back to say, "I hope you get to see whoever you came to see. Sometimes, you don't always get to."

I'm starting to wish that would be the case for me, when the man behind the desk asks me who I'm here to see.

"Michael Bellamy," I say.

He looks up, as if surprised at the name I've given him. "I don't think he's had a visitor as long as I've been here."

I nod, as if I'm aware of this, even as I think how incredibly sad that is.

"Your name?"

"Thomas Franklin."

He leans back to look at me, as if he thinks he knows me. "Have you been here before?"

"No. I haven't."

"You look awfully familiar."

I clear my throat and glance away. He goes back to his keyboard and appears to move on from my familiar face. It takes a few minutes for him to enter the information he needs from me. By the time, he buzzes someone to bring Mr. Bellamy to the visitor's area, I feel sure he could write a small book about me.

I follow an officer down a long hall and through a series of locked doors. When we reach the room, I walk inside and take a chair on my side of a glass window. A couple of minutes pass before a door on the other side opens, and Michael Bellamy is led in, wearing handcuffs.

He sits down opposite me and says, "Thank you for coming. I have to admit I kind of didn't think you would."

"I'm not sure I should have," I say. "I don't keep things from Lila, sir."

"I'm glad to hear that. Sorry I made this the first for you."

I let myself really look at him then. I look for Lila in his features, but see nothing that would make me think she's his daughter. His face is lined and tired, but it's his eyes that are hard to meet. They are eyes that carry shadows of regret, and I can only imagine how difficult it would be to have to meet such a gaze in the mirror each day. "What can I do for you, sir?"

"I wanted to meet the man my daughter married."

I hesitate, not sure what to say. "I love her very much."

He's quiet for several moments before saying, "A buddy of mine was released from here a couple of weeks ago. I asked him to see if he could find out how my daughter was doing. He sent me some pictures of her and you and Lexie. Found them online. He's also the one who sent that message to you for me. Amazing how the world out there works today. All these forms of communication and stuff."

"It is," I agree.

"I know this sounds like something I have no right to ask of you, but could you tell me about my daughter and granddaughter? What's going on in their lives? How long have you been married?"

"Less than a year," I say. "But we met years ago after a concert I did in Roanoke, Virginia. That's when—"

"Lexie came to be," he finishes.

"Yes," I say, realizing exactly how odd this conversation is.

"And you love them both?"

"More than I could ever tell you."

"That's good to know. You seem like a young man with a good head on your shoulders."

"I've had my moments. Lila has made me want to straighten up my act."

"That's what a good woman does, isn't it? Do you have pictures of Lila? Of my granddaughter?"

The question surprises me, but I nod once and say, "On my phone."

"May I see them?"

I open the photo app and turn the phone where he can see it, swiping through the pictures one by one.

I can't help but watch his face as he takes them in. A dozen emotions filter through his expression.

"Thank you," he says, when I close out the last one.

"You're welcome."

He sits silent again, as if trying to decide how to say what he wants to say.

"It's true then, what I've read about my daughter's heart?" he finally asks, his voice lowering enough that I barely hear him.

Everything inside me screams to say anything but the truth. But I can't lie to him. "The doctors have told us she will eventually need a transplant."

I can see the words hit him like individual blows. "That's just not right."

"No," I say. "It's not."

"You know the worst thing about being in this place?"

I shake my head, even though I can instantly think of at least ten things.

"All the time you have to think about how you could have done things differently."

I nod as if I understand, when I suspect I really have no way of understanding at all.

"I was a drinker then. When I first met my wife, I didn't drink. I did a stint in the Army, and that's when I started. It got a hold on me and never let go. Made me into someone I never imagined I could be. I'm not making excuses because I could have gotten myself into rehab or something, but I thought I could handle it." He glances off for a moment, and then, in a lower voice, says, "I play back so many of my memories, times we had when Lila was a little girl, and we were a happy family. It's not like you just blink one day, and it all instantly changes. I think about things I said, choices I made, and I would give anything to be able to go back and make it right again."

"Have you ever told Lila that?"

"She doesn't want to hear from me. And I don't blame her. How could I?"

"It might help her to know that you're sorry."

"I am sorry. More than I can ever express in words, but my remorse doesn't change anything. I took a life. The life of a woman I loved. The mother Lila loved."

I'm not sure what to say. What is there to say? It's true. And it's clear that he's not looking to deny any of it. I try to imagine myself in his position, but I can't get past the fact that it would have to feel like being buried alive. Whatever harsh edges he once had are now gone. What remains is a man who looks far older than his age. I think how little there is that anyone can do for him here. How there is nothing I can do for him. Except tell him about Lila. And his granddaughter.

So I do. Everything I can think of that will paint a picture of them both that he can hold onto. When I leave here, it is all he will have. But at least it will be something.

And when I get ready to go a little while later, I leave him with my cell phone number and tell him to call if he ever needs anything. He asks if I will let him know how Lila is doing from time to time.

I promise that I will.

♪

Lila

You Just Know

THERE'S AN INTUITION you develop with a person when you love them. That's the only way I can explain the feeling I have when Thomas gets home and walks into the kitchen where I'm helping Lexie with her dinner.

He kisses me hello as he always does, then kisses the top of Lexie's head and asks us about our day. He doesn't quite meet my gaze when he answers my questions about his time in the studio with CeCe and Holden.

He fills a bowl with the salad I've made and joins us at the table.

"How are you feeling, babe?" he asks.

"Good," I say, trying to sound convincing.

"Really?" he pushes.

"A little tired," I admit, leaving out the fact that I went back to bed after taking Lexie to school and stayed there until it was time to pick her up. I hate admitting it to myself, much less to him.

"Why don't I finish up dinner with Lex, get her ready for bed, and you go up and rest?"

I try to put my finger on what's different in his voice, but I actually am exhausted, and so I say, "Maybe I will, if you don't mind."

I give Lexie a kiss and go to our bedroom, sliding back under the covers where I've spent most of the day. I lie on my back, staring at the ceiling, eyes wide open as the tears seep out. I made a promise to myself somewhere along this journey that I won't indulge in self-pity. But here I am feeling sorry for myself, wishing I felt like being downstairs with my husband and daughter.

There's a truth I'm starting to realize. My heart is getting weaker. I feel it a little more every day. The reality of it is starting to seep into my mind, and I feel both weighed down and freed by it. Is this what it's like to start letting go? To give in?

I reach for the fight I felt even a couple of months ago, and I can't seem to grasp it. It's like water slipping through my fingers.

I close my eyes and drift off, coming awake to the sound of Thomas's voice saying good-night to Lexie. He comes in the bedroom, closing the door behind him and walking over to sit down on the bed beside me.

"Hey," he says. "How are you?"

"Just sleeping a little."

He presses his hand to the side of my face, rubbing his thumb across my cheek. "I'm worried about you."

"Don't be," I say, covering his hand with mine.

We sit, quiet, for a long while, until Thomas says, "There's something I need to tell you, Lila."

"What?" I ask, feeling my stomach drop, even as I realize this is the something I wondered about when he first got home.

"I went to see your father today."

I hear what he says, understand the words, and yet, I think surely I must have misunderstood him. "What?"

"I drove to the prison to see him."

I shake my head a little. "Why? Why would you do that?"

"He sent a message to our Facebook page, asking if I would come."

"But why would you?" I ask, my voice uneven.

"I didn't know what he wanted. I guess I thought he might—"

"Be able to help me?"

His silence gives me his answer.

I'm shaking now and sit up in bed. "Do you think I would ever accept help from him, even if he had any to give?"

"Lila—"

"I can't believe you went without telling me. How could you do that?"

"Please don't be upset. I knew you wouldn't want me to."

"And did he?"

"What?" he asks softly.

"Have something that will help me?"

He looks off and then meets my gaze. "No."

"So what did he want?"

"He just wanted to know about you. And Lexie. How you're doing."

"He has no right to know how we are." As the words come out, I feel a tsunami wave of anger rise up inside me. I struggle off the bed, standing to an instant wave of dizziness. I grab the corner of the nightstand just as Thomas reaches for me.

"Lila. Please. Come on. Sit back down."

"No!" I say, jerking free of his hands. "I can't believe you would do that to me."

"I'm sorry, Lila. I didn't mean to hurt you with this."

I'm crying now, full-out sobs that come from somewhere so deep inside me that I am powerless to push them back.

Thomas tries to pull me into his arms. "Please, baby," he says. "Just let me hold you."

But I don't. I can't. I have no control over my life. Over anything that is happening to me. "I'd like to be alone tonight," I say.

"Lila—"

"Please," I say. "Go. Just go."

A look of complete sadness slides across his face. I see the imploring look in his eyes, but I force myself to glance away. And he goes.

♪

Thomas

Straws

IT'S AFTER FOUR o'clock when I hear her walk into the living room. I'm on the couch, stretched out, but wide awake.

"Thomas?"

"Yeah, babe?"

"I can't sleep in there without you."

"Come here."

She walks over and lies down next to me. I wrap her up in my arms, holding her tight, and then releasing a little, for fear that I'm hurting her. "I'm so sorry, Lila," I say, kissing the side of her hair and breathing in the sweet scent of her.

She shakes her head a little, doesn't say anything for a minute or so, and then, "I understand why you went. I'm sure I would have done the same thing if it were for you."

"I should have talked to you first."

"You knew what I would say. We're both grasping at straws these days."

"Don't say that."

"It's true. I don't think there's any point in denying it."

"Lila, I can't do this without you," I say, the words cracking in half. "I can't sleep without you. I can't live without you."

She wraps her arms around me, squeezing me tight against her. She presses her face to my neck, and I feel the moisture of her tears. "I know," she says. "But you have to."

"I can't."

I cry now as I have not let myself since the beginning of this nightmare. I don't have any control over the sorrow flooding out of me. It's grief as I have never felt it, this admission that we are running out of time. That I might end up living the rest of my life on this Earth without her. It is unbearable. And I wonder how I will survive it, how I can stay here to take care of our daughter.

I hate my weakness. I'm the one who should be strong here, comforting Lila. But she is comforting me, and I let myself absorb her warmth, her love, her sorrow for everything that is happening. We lie there in the near light of morning, wrapped around each other, holding on as tight as we dare.

"Tell me about him," she says at some point.

"Are you sure?" I ask.

"Yes."

I do tell her about the place then. And how her father wanted to know everything about her and about Lexie. "He asked me to tell you something," I add at the end.

"What?" she asks softly, as if she's not sure she wants to know.

"He wanted me to tell you how sorry he is. That if he could give his life for your mother's, he would."

"But he can't."

"No."

"Can I be honest with you?"

She nods.

"I don't think he's the same man who killed your mom."

"I guess you can't be an alcoholic in prison."

"It changes people. The drinking."

"I know. But when you do an awful thing, there's no taking it back. Regardless of whether that was the real you or not."

"No. There isn't."

"He wants me to forgive him."

"I don't think he expects that."

"Then what?"

"Nothing," I say, even though it feels like there should be more.

She sighs a heavy sigh. "Do you think it's true that there's peace in forgiveness?"

I think about it for a moment, and then say, "Yeah. I think I do. As much for the forgiver, as the person being forgiven."

"I need peace," she says.

I pull her closer against me, kissing her softly on the mouth, then pushing her hair back from her face and looking into her eyes. "Then forgive. For you, baby. For you."

♪

Lila

Patchwork Moments

I FEEL BETTER the next day. It's hard to explain, but it's almost like a weight has been lifted from me. A weight I never even realized I was carrying around inside me.

Blame, I guess, is a heavy burden to indulge. Forgiving my father doesn't make me miss my mother any less, or change the fact that I long to have her in my life now, for selfish reasons, I admit. Maybe that's the hardest thing to accept about being an adult. The fact that things happen to us in this world that we simply have no control over. Or any ability to change the outcome of.

And so we just move ahead. Continue on. That's what I put my focus on now. Taking advantage of feeling better. Having a little more energy. Thomas and I go down my list of things I want to do. Little things, like taking Lexie out to Puckett's in Leiper's Fork and getting ice cream. Finding a field full of cows so she can rub their soft faces. Sitting on the front row at the Bluebird Cafe when Thomas agrees to do a round there one night for charity. Making a chocolate cake for breakfast on a Sunday morning. Taking Brownie to a nearby lake where he can fetch the Frisbee that Lexie throws in the water for him.

It's the living of these moments that makes me realize how often I have taken life for granted. How we all tend to live for the big moments, the goals we strive for, the milestones we set for ourselves.

Those can be great, I know.

But I think about a quilt my mama made for me when I was in the third grade. She took some of my baby clothes that had stains on them and cut squares from each one, putting them together in a patchwork of color and sharing with me a memory she associated with each one. They weren't big occasions, just little things like the time she

111

took me to a park and I chased the pigeons. Or the day I took my first steps. And lost my first tooth.

Like a patchwork quilt, I realize now that it's the culmination of small beautiful moments that makes the quilt of our lives so beautiful. And even though we haven't had as much time to create the fabric for the squares of ours, I know without a doubt that I will leave behind an entire quilt of beautiful moments.

♪

Thomas

Leaving the Waiting Room

YOU DON'T REALIZE that you've been living in the calm of the storm until the actual hurricane winds hit.

This happens to us on a regular Tuesday morning when we've begun to settle into a routine of life that seemed as if it would remain in a new reality of doctor's visits, medicines, and a hovering awareness of being on a list of names, of existing in a waiting room of hope.

Lila is getting dressed in the bathroom right beside me, buttoning the white shirt she's paired with jeans when I notice her hands go still. She reaches out to grab my shoulder and starts to fall just as I manage to catch her in my arms.

"Lila! Baby, what's wrong?"

Her hand is pressed to her chest, and she's gasping for air.

"Oh, God," I say. "Lila!"

I pick her up and carry her into the bedroom, laying her gently on the bed. She's trying to pull in air, and her body is rigid with the effort. I grab the phone on the nightstand and dial 911. The operator is so calm that I want to yell at her. I force myself to answer her questions and then plead for them to hurry.

I then call CeCe and ask her to come take care of Lexie. Her voice is broken when she says she'll be right over.

An eternity seems to pass during the time I wait to hear the sirens. I spend every minute of it on my knees, holding my wife's hand and praying to God that He won't really take her from me. That this has just all been some lesson I needed to learn about how precious love is. How easily we can lose. *It's true. I know it's true. Please don't take her. Please.*

♪

CECE ARRIVES before the ambulance.

113

She finds me in the bedroom with Lila, tears streaming down her face as she walks in. She drops onto her knees beside me, taking Lila's other hand and saying, "Hold on, sweetheart. Just hold on."

I don't know if Lila hears her or not. Her eyes are closed, and her breathing is terrifyingly shallow. I hear heavy footsteps in the hallway, and then Holden is there in the room, his face a mask of fear and disbelief. "What can we do, Thomas?"

"Lexie," I say. "Can you please get her dressed? Take care of her this morning?"

"Of course," CeCe says. She gets up and takes Holden's hand.

I hear the ambulance siren just as the two of them leave the room. Doors slam in the driveway, and I hear them come in. I call out, "In here, please!"

A man and a woman arrive with their equipment and begin asking me questions. I tell them everything I know about Lila's heart condition and the fact that she is on the list for a heart transplant. They work with serious expressions, and I get to my feet, standing there watching, completely helpless to do anything at all for the woman I love.

♪

THE NEXT COUPLE of hours pass in a blur of fear and uncertainty.

I wait in a small room off the emergency area at Vanderbilt. Numb and unable to think beyond my next prayer. At some point, I call my mom and tell her what has happened. She says she will get on the next available flight. Then I call Macy to let her know. She too will be here as soon as she can.

I've been in the waiting room for over an hour when Holden arrives. "CeCe is taking good care of Lexie," he says. "I want to be here for you, okay?"

I'd like to think I'm strong enough not to need it, but that's not the case. Holden steps forward and puts his arms around me, and I cry uncontrollably. He holds onto me as a brother would, the wall of support I need right now.

A woman in a white coat steps into the room. "Mr. Franklin?"

I turn to meet her questioning gaze. "Yes, that's me."

"I'm Dr. Farlington," she says, sticking out her hand. "I'm the ER chief. I've been in contact with your wife's cardiologist. We'll be admitting her to ICU. He'll speak with you there regarding her condition."

I can see the effort she is making to keep her expression neutral, to prevent any opinions about Lila's prognosis from leeching into her voice. But I feel it. The weight of her concern, the flicker of empathy in her eyes just before she turns away.

Holden steps in and puts his arms around me, as if he's determined to hold me together.

"One minute at a time, okay?" he says. "Let's just get through the next one and the next. I'm right here. I'm not going anywhere. We'll go up and talk to the doctor and go from there."

Holden's voice is laced with conviction. I know he wants to believe this is all going to be all right. That Lila's heart will somehow survive this. I want to believe that with every cell in my body. But her heart is failing. And mine is breaking.

♪

Lila

Stay

I HEAR THOMAS'S voice.

He's talking with someone I don't recognize.

Or maybe I do vaguely.

I want to open my eyes and look, but I can't find the strength to do so. My mind works for a bit, trying to place it. And then it comes to me. Dr. Maston. I'm in the hospital. They are talking about me. Words float through my consciousness. *Placement on list is critical. Transplant. Imminent need for. What is likelihood of heart becoming available? We never know. All we can do is wait.*

Someone is crying.

Thomas.

It's Thomas.

I feel the tears seep from my eyes. I want to reach out to him. Take his hand and hold on, prevent us both from falling into this well of pain and sorrow. Then I'm drifting off, a funnel of light pushing me down, down. I want to stay where I am. I don't want to leave my husband, my daughter. I want to stay. Please let me stay.

♪

Thomas

Someone Else's Chance

I SIT BY her bed for the next two days, holding her hand and talking to her about things we've done, things we want to do, things we will do. I can't eat. I can't sleep. I don't want to move from my chair because I'm afraid if I do, she'll leave me.

CeCe and Holden take turns coming in and staying with us. Macy and my mom are at the house taking care of Lexie. They send food, and CeCe tries to get me to eat. But I don't want it.

On the second afternoon of Lila being in the ICU, CeCe asks me to step outside the room for just a minute. I'm reluctant to do so, but I hear the worry in her voice.

"I went by your house to check on Lexie. There was a reporter at the door. He wanted to know if it's true that Lila is in critical condition. He caught me off guard, and I might have said more than you would want me to. I'm sorry. I probably shouldn't have said anything at all."

"It's okay," I say, pulling her to me and hugging her tight.

"Can I be selfish for a minute?" she asks.

"Yeah."

"Maybe the publicity will make it more likely that she'll get a donor."

"She wouldn't want it that way," I say. "She wouldn't want to come before someone else for any reason other than that it's her turn. She wouldn't want to take someone else's chance."

"I know," CeCe says, pressing her face to my chest.

I feel her tears and then my own as they slide down my face.

"I just feel so helpless," she says softly.

I rub my hand across her hair, and we hold onto each other, saying nothing because there is nothing to say.

♪

THE ARTICLE APPEARS online late that afternoon.

**WIFE OF COUNTRY MUSIC STAR NEEDS NEW HEART
SOON**

The article goes on to talk about the fact that Lila is on the list for a transplant, that time becomes the determining factor in cases such as hers. The sight of those words fills me with a rage that ignites with such ferocity that I think it will completely consume me. It's not that it's inaccurate. Or that they don't have the right to put our personal life out for public consumption. It's the fact that everything they have said is true. And I can't make it not true.

♪

Thomas

An Unusual Request

I'M HOLDING LILA'S hand, leaning forward with my head next to her shoulder, listening to her breathing, afraid to stop listening. If I do, she might let go altogether. Part of my brain registers the night sounds of the other patients in the ICU. Nurses come and go, giving injections, changing IV bags, glancing at me with sympathetic eyes.

My phone buzzes in my shirt pocket, and I jump at the unexpectedness of it. I sit up and pull it out, glancing at the screen. RED ONION STATE PRISON.

I feel an immediate stab of guilt for not having called Lila's father and told him what was going on. I had promised him I would, but somehow, it's been the last thing on my mind. I swipe the screen and put the phone to my ear, stepping outside the ICU to say, "Hello."

"This is Warden McPherson at the Red Onion State Prison in Virginia. I'm trying to reach Thomas Franklin."

"Yes," I say, my voice cautious. "This is he."

"I'm afraid I'm calling with bad news, Mr. Franklin. Michael Bellamy ended his life in his cell a short while ago."

I hear the words, but find that they won't quite process, the edges fuzzy and incomprehensible. "What? But I just saw him—"

"You're his son-in-law, correct?"

"Yes."

"I'm very sorry, Mr. Franklin. He did leave a note with an unusual request."

I shake my head, trying to focus. "What is it?"

"He wanted his daughter to have his heart. There's a note here for you. Would you like for me to read it?"

"Yes, please," I say, barely able to get the words out.

He clears his throat and begins reading. "Dear Thomas, I just learned of how sick Lila is. Through the friend I told you about when you were here, I've tried to find out as much as I could about what makes a heart transplant possible. I do remember from Lila's childhood medical records that she and I are the same blood type. Body size is apparently important, and since I'm not an overly large man, I hope this will make my heart compatible. Time will be the other factor. I had some help from the cell mate next to me. It was his job to get a guard to my cell as soon after I leave this world as possible. I truly pray that it will work out. I'm afraid from this point it will be up to you. But knowing how much you love her, I am sure no one will try harder. Sincerely, Michael Bellamy."

I am so stunned that I can't bring myself to speak for several moments. I finally say, "Can we make this happen?"

"We'll do our best from this end," he says, compassion softening his voice. "Can you put me in touch with her doctor?"

"Yes. Yes." My legs threaten to lose the ability to hold me up. But I force myself to run. Down the hall, calling for help as I go. It isn't until I hand the phone to one of the transplant doctors that I drop to my knees in the middle of the hospital floor and cry for joy. And terror. And hope.

♪

Lila

Worth Living

Three Weeks Later

SO OFTEN, BLESSINGS don't feel like blessings at first.

To wake up from surgery and be told that I had a new heart felt like something that couldn't possibly be true. I hadn't believed that it could really happen. But it had. And my father had died to make it so.

I don't know that there's any way to explain everything I felt upon learning this. Anger came first. I didn't want his heart. His heart was flawed. It had loved my mother. And hated my mother. And now it was inside me.

I cried for a full day, unable to stop, despite Thomas's every effort to console me. The doctors had finally given me something to make me sleep, and I sank into its escape with utter thankfulness.

When I woke up the next morning, it was to the sight of my daughter's face. She sat in her chair by my bed. Thomas was helping her draw me a picture. It was a wonderfully colorful drawing of our family. Thomas, me, Lexie, Brownie. The sun was shining from a blue sky, and we were all happy. Lexie's smile was the biggest.

When she looked up to see me watching her, she dropped the picture to the floor and leaned forward to hug me, tighter than she ever had. She didn't let go for a long time, and it was then that I realized how much she needed me to be here. And that my father had given me that gift.

Three full weeks have passed before I can bring myself to pull the envelope from beneath my pillow. Thomas had given it to me after the surgery, but I refused to read it. Today, I wait until he takes Lexie to the cafeteria. The envelope is still sealed, my father's handwriting on the front. I pull the piece of blue-lined paper out and unfold it.

Dear Lila,

I know you will never willingly accept what I've asked to do. I can only hope you will not be left to make the choice. I understand completely why you would reject this heart of mine. It is as imperfect as a heart can get. But it is my prayer that it will allow you to live the life of love you deserve with the good man you've married and the beautiful daughter you made together. I don't expect you to ever forgive me. I ruined the life I had with your mother and you. I ruined it all. What I am doing will never in any way make up for that. But maybe it will allow you to see that I am so very sorry. I'm so sorry, Lila. May you be well. And happy.

Daddy

My tears drop onto the page, blurring some of the words. I fold the paper and put it back in the envelope, feeling my heart swell with the most painful mixture of sadness and forgiveness. I know in a way that I cannot even explain that he meant every word of what he said. This heart of his is now this heart of mine. It is a heart that asked to be forgiven. A heart that can love and feel gratitude. And I do. Feel all of that. I am here with more love in my life than I can ever imagine deserving.

My heart is beating. And I will not waste a moment of this life I've been left here to live by asking it to feel remorse, regret, or resentment.

This heart will love and be loved.

That is the only life worth living.

♪

Next: Nashville – Book Eight – R U Serious

Books by Inglath Cooper

My Italian Lover – What If – Book One
Fences
Dragonfly Summer – Book Two – Smith Mountain Lake Series
Blue Wide Sky – Book One – Smith Mountain Lake Series
That Month in Tuscany
Crossing Tinker's Knob
Jane Austen Girl
Good Guys Love Dogs
Truths and Roses
Nashville – Book Ten – Not Without You
Nashville – Book Nine – You, Me and a Palm Tree
Nashville – Book Eight – R U Serious
Nashville – Book Seven – Commit
Nashville – Book Six – Sweet Tea and Me
Nashville – Book Five – Amazed
Nashville – Book Four – Pleasure in the Rain
Nashville – Book Three – What We Feel
Nashville – Book Two – Hammer and a Song
Nashville – Book One – Ready to Reach
On Angel's Wings
A Gift of Grace
RITA® Award Winner John Riley's Girl
A Woman With Secrets
Unfinished Business
A Woman Like Annie
The Lost Daughter of Pigeon Hollow
A Year and a Day

Get in Touch With Inglath Cooper

Email: inglathcooper@gmail.com
    Facebook – Inglath Cooper Books
    Instagram – inglath.cooper.books
    Pinterest – Inglath Cooper Books
    Twitter – InglathCooper
    Join Inglath Cooper's Mailing List and get a FREE ebook! Good Guys Love Dogs!

Made in the USA
Middletown, DE
29 January 2021